The

Bitch

Madam

IKE KEEN

Paperback-Press
an imprint of A & S Publishing
A & S Holmes, Inc.

ISBN: 0692307613
ISBN-13: 978-0-692-30761-8

ACKNOWLEDGEMENTS

I'd like to thank Norma Eaton for proofreading this book. Good job. Thanks to all of the writing groups I'm in for helping me hone my skills. Special thanks to Paperback-Press for helping me get my books to the readers.

TABLE OF CONTENTS

IN THE BEGINNING

The city streets are the same everywhere. The good, the bad, the homeless seem to all come to the city streets at one time or the other. These streets might not be anything like St. Louis or Kansas City, but they still hold the same attitude, good during the daylight, bad during the night.

It was two in the morning, the temperature outside five degrees above zero. A hell of a night to commit a murder since most people were at home in bed snuggled up to someone next to them, which was what I was doing when the phone rang.

I slapped at it, grabbed at it as it flipped off the cradle onto the floor with a thump. I grunted and grabbed at it again, then slid over the edge of the bed, a voice coming to me as the damned thing bounced out of my reach, me onto the floor with it, Shelly squealed as my feet thumped her ass on the way over. I grabbed the damned thing, sat up and growled into the receiver.

"Who the hell is this?"

"You better come down here Max." I recognized Pat's voice on the other end, "Bruce Stedman's ticket has been punched."

"So why call me?" I snapped as I pushed myself up from the floor.

"We found your card in what was left of his jacket. Just get here as soon as you can." Then there was a click, the dial tone hummed in my ear.

I stood and dressed, Shelly rolled over rising up on one elbow, the cover slid down to her waist. Shelly is a sexy woman, tall and leggy with a lot of curves and a set of sweater puppies that keeps my attention.

"Who was that?" she asked as I pulled on my socks and shoes.

"That was Pat, somebody punched Bruce Stedman's ticket."

"The same Stedman who hired you last month?"

I nodded as I slid into my rig, liberated my .45 from its home under my arm, ejected the clip and checked it then slid it home, jacked a shell in the chamber and let the hammer down, stowing it back under my arm. Stedman had hired me to shadow his wife; he suspected she was catting around with a buddy of his who was a salesman in the used car business. He told me she had always favored the other guy over him because he was a little more robust than Stedman. He wanted proof of just how robust.

I'd only been on the case for a couple of days and from what I'd seen, Stedman's wife was not stepping out, she was more like stepping in. Every Tuesday and Thursday, she went to Russo's Italian Restaurant, stayed about four hours then left. Russo's is only a front, the upstairs a restaurant, the downstairs a gambling den, one that every time Pat raids finds nothing more than little old ladies playing bingo for prizes.

I leaned down, kissed Shelly on the cheek, then told her to go back to sleep as I headed toward the front door pulled my trench coat on and braced myself for the cold.

CHAPTER 1

The sun was just peeking up above the buildings on Commercial Street when I pulled up to the curb. A few cops, older men who were past draft age, blocked the street entrance to the alley. One of them was Art Gibson, a throwback from the old days when they used to get confessions with rubber hoses and bright lights.

"Pat's waitin' for ye." His Irish brogue came out in thick clouds of steam. I nodded as he stepped aside, a couple of reporters trying to squeeze in behind me. Gibson tossed an arm up giving the reporters a growl and told them if they tried that again they would be reporting this story from a jail cell.

Floodlights were trained on the body of Stedman slumped between two trashcans. Three feet above him a bloody spatter decorated the wall and its trail followed him down to where he sat, brains and blood spatters dotting his suit jacket. He'd been beaten first, his face swollen, one eye closed completely, his lips split, a couple of teeth missing. Bruce's clothes were torn and dirty, blotches of mud stained his pants and jacket. I took a step closer and knelt in front of him Allen Ross the current M.E. gave me the eye as I did.

"So what's the skinny?" I knelt beside the body.

"Besides me getting here before you did?" I gave him a smirk and he grinned at me. He hated it when I got to a crime scene before he did because I tend to look the deceased over before he does, meaning I move the body some. Aggravates the hell out of him.

"How long's he been dead?" I ignored his quip, scanned the body from head to toe and noticed some dark blotches on his bloody shirt.

"Probably four or five hours," Ross mouthed at me as he started to work the body over again.

"His jacket looks like it's been cut?" I pointed to the long slices in his coat. "And the dark stuff looks like oil."

"Very good Max." Ross nodded, his voice had a little sarcastic ring to it. "He was beaten before he was brought here, the bruises probably a couple of days old. The oil feels too fine to be motor oil so I'm guessing he was beaten someplace where they either run or store machinery."

I gave him my 'you're an asshole' look for his tone of voice, then took a pencil from my pocket and lifted Stedman's jacket open a bit, touched the oily spot and rubbed my fingers together, the oil smooth as silk to the touch. The inner lining of his jacket had been sliced open along with the outsides and searched in a hurry, pieces of it scattered on the ground beside him. I let the jacket flap I was holding drop, stood then stepped back looking at the wall and blood spatter.

"Someone dug the bullet out of the wall." Ross said. I leaned in closer for a better look. One of the uniforms shifted the floodlight on the spot and a muttered 'I'll be damned came from my mouth'. In the gore was a faint print.

"Yeah." Pat came up behind me. "They weren't too careful, leaving a print in the blood. One of my boys lifted it and is headed back to run it now."

"What about the slug?" I asked him.

"We thought maybe the two rummies dug it out for a souvenir. As to frisking them?" Pat chuckled and shrugged.

"Who found him?" I asked as I turned toward Pat.

"Lester," Pat said.

"Stinky Lester?" I made a face and snarled my nose.

"Yeah, he and his buddy Keller." Pat nodded. Stinky Lester as he was referred to is one of the more colorful winos around here. Mean as hell when he needs to be and loud, his voice reminding you of a bull bellowing in the back pasture. It's said he has worn the same clothes since he turned up on the street here ten years ago, that it's been that long since he has taken a bath. No wonder none of the cops on duty wanted to search him. I wouldn't.

"Have you talked to him?" I eyed Pat and chuckled.

"Yeah, for as long as I could stand it. Geez, if he ever takes a bath he'll die of exposure," Pat laughed shaking his head. I laughed and asked where Lester was. Pat jerked his thumb toward the other end of the alley so I headed that way.

Lester was leaning against the wall at the mouth of the alley, a uniform giving the fellow plenty of room. The smell reached me before I got within three feet of him. He was an average sized man, his hair long and covered by a stocking cap that was dark colored and dirty. He was dressed in layers of clothes, at least three, the outer layer crusty with dirt. His shoes were in fair shape, the leather cracked in places, the laces looked fairly new.

Pat was right, if he ever took a bath, his skin would go into shock. He turned and looked at me, the dirt on him, I swear to god, flaked off his neck as he grunted and locked his brown eyes on me.

"I already told the cops everything I know shamus." Stinky glared at me.

"Everything?" I held a fin up in front of his eyes.

"Well, maybe not all..." A smile split his lips as he reached for the fin. I jerked it back and shook my head no.

"Information first, then you get the money." Lester grunted his breath worse than his body odor.

"Me and Keller we heard the shot that killed him. We were coming up on the alley and we saw this guy holding the other one against the wall. The guy yelled at the guy against the wall to hand it over or he wouldn't live another day. Then we heard the gunshot so Keller ran for a cop while I waited, I could hear the guy cuss under his breath and cloth ripping. He beat it when he heard the sirens."

"Did you see the guy?"

"Hey, I didn't look; he had a gun and I like livin' too much."

I nodded and handed him the fiver. Lester grinned; his teeth blackened stumps as he kissed the five then shoved it in his pocket. I walked back to where Pat was, pulled out a cigar and lit up, drew deep and hoped it would purge the smell from my nose.

"He tell you anything different?" Pat asked.

"No, probably what he told you." I related what Lester had said.

Pat gave me a lopsided grin and asked, "So you paid him five dollars for that?"

"No, I paid five dollars to look at his hands and I bet when you get the print back it'll belong to Lester."

Pat grinned and nodded; he had seen the same thing but thought maybe I could get some more information he couldn't which was sometimes true. I looked at Ross who was digging a fin out of his pocket and handed it to Wendell his assistant, Wendell grinned, winked at me and stuffed it in his pocket as he went to get the rubber bag to haul Stedman away.

"You must be losing your touch," Ross said as he watched Wendell walk away.

"Better than losing a fiver to your assistant," I

chuckled. He grunted and turned around, yelling at Wendell to hurry the hell up. He didn't have all day.

CHAPTER 2

Like I said, the print on the wall belonged to Lester so Pat had him picked up and hauled in. They brought him in screaming and kicking, tossed him in the drunk tank and four officers stripped him, a fire hose used to blast the dirt off of him. Lester was *not* pleased.

He was given new clothes then taken to one of the interrogation rooms, his hair a tangled mess but at least clean. Pat and I stood outside the door, the four cops laughed and told us that Lester actually passed out while they were hosing him down.

"I was close," Pat laughed. When we stepped into the 'fish tank' as some of the older hoods called it because of the observation room on the other side of the one way glass, Lester started screaming at us.

"Torturers, masochists," he bellowed at the top of his lungs. "Bullies of the Inquisition!"

I picked up a chair and sat it close to Lester, straddled it then leaned on the back and tipped my fedora back as I gave him a nasty stare.

"You through yelling?" Lester grunted and shrugged

his shoulders. Since he was clean I leaned in closer, a sneer crossed my lips as I spoke to him.

"Well then," I nodded to Pat who dropped a file in front of him and opened it. "We found a print on the wall in the splatter of Stedman's blood. Guess who it belonged to?"

Lester gave me a nasty look, his lips curled back from his black stumps. He tensed, his body tightened up and his eyes spit sparks. I gave him a nasty grin then slipped my hand under my coat, my voice dropped to a whispered hiss.

"That print could get you Ol' Sparky Stinky. *Your* print was the only one at the scene in the victim's blood so drop the act and level with us or Pat here is gonna charge you with murder."

For a moment Lester glared at me then his eyes slowly lost their fire and his body relaxed. He cleared his throat and leaned on the table as he spoke.

"I did look," he mouthed in a quiet voice, "right after Keller took off after the cops. The guy was cutting the other guy's jacket open. I got a look at him."

"And he looked like?" Pat asked.

"Tall guy, he had on a nice suit, looked like a gray pin stripe, but that's only a guess since the alley was only half lit. He also had on one of them German hats, the kind with the brim curled up around the edges."

"A Homburg?" I said.

"Yeah." Lester nodded.

"Did you see his face?" Lester shook his head and let out a slow breath which I wish he had kept in.

"Not very well, but he did have a scar on his jaw, it shined white like it was painted with glow paint and it was jagged, ran from behind his ear to about an inch from his chin. He also had an accent because he cussed in it while he cut up the guy's coat. Sounded like he was German. Oh, he wore gloves, black or dark gray gloves. Like I said; the alley wasn't too well lit. Finally he stood, cussed a blue streak then took the knife he used on the coat and dug the slug out of the wall and took off. That was a few minutes before the cops came."

"When he was out of the alley, I went to see if the guy had maybe survived but he was dead as a door nail when I leaned down to check on him. I didn't know I had put my hand in the goo on the wall until after I went back to the mouth of the alley and saw my hand was stained red. I wiped most of it off on a rag I found. I thought I got it all wiped off. Guess I didn't. So when do I get my clothes back?"

"You don't, and if I was you I'd put this money in a bank." Pat closed the file then tossed a manila envelope on the table in front of Lester.

"Those clothes *were* my bank!" Lester yelled then started sobbing. Pat shook his head as we stepped outside and closed the door.

"How much was in that envelope?" Lester was sobbing his heart out and moaning about his clothes as Pat gave a little shrug and spoke.

"Over a thousand dollars, most of it ones pinned to each layer of clothing. That's why it took four of them to get his clothes off; he kept screaming he was being robbed."

****

The thermometer had reached a sultry ten degrees and the wind had kicked up outside tossing trash and other loose items around that weren't froze to the street. Even in the bitter cold, people were out and about, going from store to store in a hurry. Another gust of wind rattled the front window of Shelly's office where I sat. A couple of papers sailed by as two girls walked past fighting their coats back down around their legs, two solider boys followed behind them grinning.

Around eleven Shelly bounced in, dressed like an Eskimo and stomped her feet on the floor. She moved to the radiator and held her hands over it for a moment, then took off her gloves and held them over it again.

"That damned cab driver." She turned and backed up to the heater her eyes snapping sparks.

"A problem kitten?" I dropped my feet off the corner of her desk and leaned forward on it.

"A cab comes and picks me up. About halfway here the car starts spraying steam and dies. He crawls out, lifts the hood and starts cussing, kicked the tires and banged his fists on the fender." Shelly rubbed her butt, her eyes narrowing.

"Let me guess. His car froze up?" I was trying to keep the grin off my face but without much luck.

"Damned right it did so I get out and tell him I'll walk the rest of the way. He steps in front of me, grabs my arm as I try to walk around him and tells me I have to pay my fare. I told him to forget it and he gets real close, tells me he will call a cop if I don't so I gave him something to call a cop about."

Her face was red; her eyes flashed as I chuckled and shook my head, "And did he?"

"Did he what?" She snapped at me.

"Call a cop?"

"He couldn't, he was too busy rolling on the ground holding his crotch!"

I couldn't help it; I laughed. Shelly has a hell of a temper, one that whoever is in the firing line of suffers the consequences. She huffed and pulled off her coat and scarf, tossed them on the coat rack then stepped up beside me, my butt leaving the chair before she should get physical with me.

"Laugh all you want hotshot. He yelled he was gonna sue me, that I had probably ruined his family life." She snapped at me as she plopped down in the chair and turned toward me. "And with his looks maybe that is a good thing!"

I wiped my eyes and told her not to worry; I'd call Stan down at the cab company and tell him what happened. She huffed again then turned toward her desk, took a file and slapped it down in front of her. I walked back into my office, poured her a cup of coffee, took it out and set it on her desk. She mumbled thanks then sighed, grabbed my hand before I got away and gave it a squeeze. I leaned down and kissed her forehead then went back into my office, a picture of the guy on the frozen street rolling around holding his nuts and groaning making me laugh again.

I poured myself a cup of coffee and sat down at my desk and cleared a spot on top of it to set the mug. Unlike Shelly's, mine is a mess but if you move anything I can't find it. As they say, everything in its place. I mulled over what Stinky said about the guy having a scar that glowed. Somewhere back in the pits of my mind a thought crawled forward so I stood and went to my file cabinet, pulled open a drawer and thumbed through the files until I came to the one I wanted. I opened it; the mug shot of the guy Stinky described stared back at me.

The name on the file was Fredrick "The Butcher" Striker. He's the go to guy when someone wants something nasty done, something like getting a guy to spill his guts if he had something someone wanted or Striker would spill them for him. Stedman had something someone wanted. I tossed the file on my desk and called the Station and asked if Pat was around. The dispatcher said he wasn't in but he could contact him by radio if I wanted him to. I told him to do that and tell him to come see me.

Thirty minutes later Pat waltzed into my office. I told him to set down as soon as he unwrapped then handed him the file. Pat read it for a few minutes then looked up at me, his eyes narrowed a little as he asked, "This is a police file.

How the hell did you get it?"

"I've got connections. That's the man you need to be looking for." I pointed at the file.

"Uh-huh, so what makes you think this is the man who offed Stedman?"

"As you and I both know, Freddy is the one who is called in when someone needs to be persuaded to tell what they know. His M.O. is torture then a bullet in the head whether he gets what he wants or not."

"Okay, so Stedman had something that someone wanted but what and who?"

"That's the sixty-four dollar question I'm going to find the answer to."

"So you got me here for this?"

"No, I need you to arrange a meeting for me with someone in the county lock up. Someone who can tell me what Stedman had and who hired Striker to get it."

Pat grunted and closed the file, tossed it on my desk as I wrote down the name on a piece of paper and handed it to him. He shook his head as he read it, stuffed it in his pocket then stood.

"Anything else Sherlock?"

I shook my head as he walked to my office door, stopped then turned toward me.

"By the way, I got a call from Stan, said one of his cab drivers had a run in with a crazy lady, she kicked him in the balls after he tried to get her to pay her fare after his cab froze up," his voice low, a slow smile crossed his face, "The driver wanted to have assault charges filed against her until I told Stan about those parking tickets the driver hadn't paid. Stan said he would remind him."

"Thanks," I chuckled.

"No problem. Just watch your ass on this one Max; if it is Striker he is bad news." He opened the door and walked out.

"Consider it watched," I saluted him.

Striker was not a fellow to be underestimated, the man a sadistic piece of shit whose reputation in the criminal world was one of fear and loathing. I had heard many tales of his torture methods, men and women, especially women, being taken to the doors of death only to be pulled back and made to suffer more of his tortures.

Yeah, I'll watch my ass because I want to see if Freddy boy can take it like he dishes it out.

CHAPTER 3

The county jail takes up the bottom floor of the courthouse basement. To get to it, you go to the east side, down a ramp and through a steel door to the front desk. There is deputy there to take reports from citizens and if he isn't doing that, he's reading the Police Gazette. Behind the counter that runs the length of the room, a few desks sit, deputies hunched over typewriters, some talking on the phone or just talking to each other.

Behind the desks to the right is the drunk tank where the bums and winos and other unfortunate souls are caged together after a night of revelry. The floor of the cell slopes to the center and after a night of drunks being tossed in to sleep it off, among other things, the floor is hosed down. To the left are ten holding cells, the extra bad boys held in there, some for a few nights until the boys from the pen come down to pick them up after their sentencing, others serving time for minor offenses like stealing or selling moonshine.

One of the fellows I wanted to talk to was serving three months for assaulting his brother-in-law with a cleaver hacked the brother-in-law's ear off after he caught him heavy petting with his wife. The brother-in-law didn't press charges but told them just to put him in the lockup for a couple of months to cool off. The judge being a close relative to the brother-in-law agreed. I hear the wife and the brother-in-law ran off to California.

Carter Hamilton sat in his cell reading a detective magazine, his feet propped up on the lower rail of the bottom bunk, his chair rocked back on two legs. He grinned when he saw me and nodded. A deputy opened the cell and stepped in, walked over to Carter and started to kick the chair out from under him. In two steps I was beside the deputy, my hand clamped down on his shoulder and spun him around. His nightstick was halfway out before he stopped, my eyes blazed into his, a nasty smile on my face. He was about to go ahead and draw the nightstick when a voice sounded behind us, a low, drawling voice that carried authority.

"I wouldn't do that if I was you Jody," the voice said, "You might just be walkin' out of here with it shoved up your ass."

My nasty smile widened as I slowly nodded. Jody flicked his eyes behind me, shoved the nightstick home and walked around me, his eyes never leaving mine as I followed him. Deputy Burks was standing in the cell doorway, chuckling and shaking his head.

"Call when you're done." He turned and walked away talking to the deputy as he went. I nodded and walked over to the lower bunk, sat down on it shaking my head as I pushed on the mattress with my hand.

"You sleep on this thing?" I asked Carter giving the mattress a slap. He shook his head.

"Nope, sleep on the top one, my cell mate is in the hospital because he didn't want to trade places. Seems one night he just fell out of the top bunk, broke his arm." Carter winked. Carter isn't a big man, just an average sized fellow but he was raised in the hills outside the city, his pappy trying to farm a rocky patch of land that grew only a little corn which was then used to feed the old man's still. Carter had two brothers, both of them bigger that Carter so he had to learn how to use his fists plus other, less honorable ways to keep from getting his ears peeled back.

I laughed and Carter let the other two legs of his chair down, marked his place in the magazine then leaned toward me.

"What's on your mind Max?"

"The Butcher."

Carter leaned back in his chair again and shook his head. Carter was the man to go to when you wanted any dope on what was going on in the organization. In reality he was a planted informant by the Feds and if the boys in the organization ever found out *he* would be planted. Of course the Feds could have gotten him off from the cleaver incident but that might blow his cover so he was serving time to satisfy the big boys.

"The skinny is Biscayne called him in." Carter laced his hands behind his head and eyed me.

"Biscayne, why?"

"Well, seems that Russo's office was broken into a few nights back and something was stolen that was very valuable, a notebook, one that if it falls into the hands of the law will put him and a few others in the pen for a long time.

"And Biscayne wants it for?"

"Leverage, there are some pretty important names in that book, Russo was ignorant enough to keep tabs on all those names, their dislikes and *detailed* likes."

"Oh brother," I mumbled under my breath.

"Yeah." Carter nodded.

"So who took it?"

"Word is it was that fellow they found dead in the alley but it wasn't him."

I leaned forward some more, my eyes locked with his, and asked again, "So who, damn it!"

"His wife, Monica Stedman, she was supposed to have liberated the notebook right out from under Russo's nose and slipped away with it. Biscayne found out about it and called in The Butcher to get it before Russo could."

"So Biscayne and Russo's hoods are both looking for it?" I shook my head leaning back.

"Yep, the Feds would also like to get their hands on it too but they've got bigger fish to fry right now with the war and all."

"Any idea where Freddy might be hold up?"

"Couldn't tell ya." Carter shook his head. "Be careful around this one Max. He likes pain. The more he gives the crazier he gets."

"Sounds like a good candidate for a lead cocktail."

"Uh-huh, just be sure you deliver that cocktail between his eyes, wounding him only makes him angry."

I stood as Carter let the legs of his chair back on all fours and picked up his magazine off the lower bunk and nodded a goodbye as I walked out of his cell, another jailer standing a few feet away. He touched the bill of his cap as I passed and went back out into the squad room, Pat, Burks and the dumbass deputy talking together.

He gave me a hard look and tried to step in front of me. Burks cleared his throat and the deputy stopped and glared. I stepped up to the group and looked over my shoulder at the deputy, grinned and stuck my tongue out at him. Yeah, it was kiddish but it got the desired effect. His face went red and he started to say something but Burks cut him off.

"Strawberry, don't you have some paperwork to finish?" Burks asked. I jerked my head back around toward Burks and chuckled.

Burks smiled, "When he first came here the boys ribbed him a lot, nicknamed him dingle berry."

"A name like that can give a man a complex." I glanced over my shoulder again, Strawberry shuffling papers, glaring at me.

"Yeah, it can. You find out what you needed to know?"

I nodded and conveyed to the two what Carter had said to me, Burks the only one in the sheriff's department who knew the real story about Carter, and the only one trusted.

"Damn, leave it to a woman to cause a man a lot of grief." Burks shook his head, making a clicking sound with his tongue.

"Yeah." I pulled out a cigar and lit up. "Of course some women are worth the trouble."

Both men nodded. Pat and I were about to leave when one of the other deputies yelled at us.

"Captain Peterson, your dispatcher just called, you got another one over on Porter Street, a burglary, a woman dead."

He came across the floor and handed Pat a piece of paper, both of us read it then made tracks toward the door.

****

Porter Street was over on the northwest side of town, the neighborhood slightly run down but not so much that is was considered trashy. A couple of the houses could fall in that category but they were vacant with for rent signs nailed to the front porch waiting for the next renter to come along and do what the landlord wouldn't, fix the place up. Two cop cars and a cruiser blocked the street, a small crowd gathered gawking.

Monica had been beaten like her husband only beaten more viciously, her driver's license found on the floor beside her bed. She had been a very pretty woman, tall and curvy, good sized knockers and a face that reminded you of

Lana Turner. She had been tied to the bed, legs to the lower bed posts, hands to the upper, nobody had heard her scream because someone had put cotton in her mouth and used packing tape to hold it in place.

She had been beaten first, the skin around her mouth red and irritated where after a good thumping they had pulled it loose to get her to answer questions. I suspect more cotton was added later when her captor decided to work her over for the fun of it, Ross using a pair of long handled tweezers to pull the rest of it out of her throat which was the cause of her death. Evidently she hadn't talked because the house was torn apart, chair cushions ripped up, stuffing tossed about, pictures yanked from the walls and torn from their frames, even the bed she was on had been slit open and searched.

Monica herself wasn't good to look at for along with the bruising she had been flayed, strips of her skin laying on either side of her in neat rows. Her breasts were cut to ribbons and her face was missing her eyes, well not missing, just pulled out, cut off the stems and placed at the head of each row of flesh strips. This went beyond sick, this was psychotic.

I went back out into the living room, Pat talking to one of the patrolmen who had gotten here first, his face pale, and his hands shaking. He was leaned over the porch rail when Pat arrived. Pat had asked him if he was up to describing what he saw first when he came into the bedroom and each time he made a dash for the porch and hugged the rail. This was his third attempt and I felt like he wasn't gonna make this one either.

"Jesus," his voice broke a little as he glanced at the bedroom. "Sweet Jesus I ain't ever…"

He didn't finish this time either, his hand clamped over his mouth as he barreled out, this time into the yard. Pat shook his head, flipped his notebook shut and walked over to where I stood, his face a little pale itself.

"You think they found what they were looking for?" Pat glanced around the room and shook a cigarette out of the deck he took out of his pocket.

"They?" I looked at him.

"Don't tell me you think one guy did all this?" There was a surprised look on his face and I nodded as I stepped away from him and moved around the room, watching the floor as I let my eyes take in all the mess. Hell yes, only one guy had done this and that guy was Striker. The place had been tossed, but tossed methodically just like he tortured his victims, piled in rows in the center of the room, four to be exact and piled in cone shapes. That was another of his traits mentioned in his file. I went from one pile to the next, poked at it with my foot and when something looked interesting I used the eraser end of a pencil to separate it from the rest of the mess to look it over. Books had been ripped apart, glass vases shattered but the smaller stuff was just tossed, a couple of pieces, angels, placed on the floor in one piece.

I went out to the kitchen and it was the same, pots and pans in one pile, jars opened then closed and tossed on the floor and stacked in the shape of a pyramid. I went over to the cellar door and opened it, flicked on the light and found it was out, or so I thought. I went down a few steps and pecked at it, it was loose so I screwed it in. I walked on down and at the bottom was another light hanging from the ceiling this one loose too. I gave it a turn and it came on, the light pooled out so far, the places it didn't reach cast in shadowy darkness.

Nothing had been touched down here, no cone shaped piles in the floor, just cobwebs and my footprints in the accumulated dust on the steps. I grinned, went back upstairs flicked off the switch and closed the door. Pat stepped into the kitchen just as I did. I paused for a moment, rubbed my chin and looked back at the door.

"Anything down there?" He nodded toward the door.

"Nada." I shook my head but felt like I had missed something.

"I'll have the lab boys check it anyway." I shrugged, walked around him back into the living room and suddenly realized our friend The Butcher was afraid of the dark, something I filed away in my mind for further reference as I walked on through the living room and out the door. That something I missed wasn't Freddy's fear of darkness, but something else, something that was gnawing at the edges of my brain, laughing at me the more I tried to pin it down.

****

I rode with Pat back to his office, called Shelly to let her know I was still alive and told her not to worry about going back home tonight; we would camp out in the apartment above the office until the weather warmed a little, which was probably going to be in the spring.

Before I met Shelly I had lived in the apartment which also served as my office until the dress shop on the ground floor became vacant. Then the apartment was nothing but a storeroom that I cleaned out, cleaned up, put in a bed, a dresser and a desk, had a bathroom installed in the closet which held only a sink and a toilet, just right for a single man and his occasional over nighter. When Shelly came into my life, I had to make some alterations, one being getting a bigger dresser, the one I used small, holding a few pair of boxers, some undershirts and four shirts.

The dresser was still there, but another one had been hauled up, this one taking up a big space along the east wall, a mirror attached to it and enough drawers to hold, as she called them, her delicates, plus other stuff a woman can't do without. The other dresser was used for my underwear, a couple more shirts besides what I had before, and sheets of which I only had one set, now there were four, the bed getting a change once a week whether it needed it or not and the room cleaned.

Once I asked her why she went up there and moved the dust around. She just gave me a funny look and went on with what she was doing so I let it drop, never asked again which I was told was the right thing to do. Go figure.

I hung up then plopped down in the chair beside Pat's desk, inspected the butt end of my cigar which had turned into a soggy mess, dropped it in the trashcan and pulled out another one to replace it. Pat talked on the other phone with Ross the city's M.E., grunted into the receiver and nodded as he scribbled on a pad. When he hung up, he sat and stared at the pad for a few moments, made a couple more notations and nodded.

"Well?" I shifted in the chair as he tossed the pad over toward me and pointed.

"The blade was a thin job, sharp as a razor. Ross said it was probably custom made. Fits our boy The Butcher." He leaned back in his chair shaking a Lucky from his deck. "Whatever this notebook has in it is deadly to whoever Striker thinks has it."

"Yeah which he hasn't found *who* has it yet." I scanned the pad then tossed it back. "Every room in that house was tossed; if it had been there Freddy would have found it."

"So what did Stedman do with it?"

"Who knows, maybe he handed it off to someone he trusted or it's still in the house somewhere?"

"Huh-uh, my people went over the house with a fine tooth comb and didn't turn up any hidey holes or hidden safes. What about where he worked?"

"The bank, I doubt it, too much of a chance it would be found by someone else. You know how old Barker likes to snoop through his employees desks."

"Maybe Stedman rented a safety deposit box?"

"That's a possibility."

"Then we'll get a warrant and…"

I shook my head no and Pat blew smoke at me and eyed me. A grin spread across my face as I stood.

"I know that grin." He scowled at me and leaned forward. "What'd you plan to do?"

"Just to check to see if he has rented one?" I walked to the door and pulled it open, Pat's eyes narrowed and he pointed at me.

"If old man Barker calls me…"

"Trust me, he won't." I opened the door and stepped out. I heard Pat mutter something about me and how he was gonna deck me if I put old man Barker on his ass. I laughed and headed for the door.

CHAPTER 4

Samuel J. Barker had been president of the Citizen's Bank for over thirty five years. It was one door east of my office and has a big clock on the front that is always five minutes fast. Barker had started as a teller and worked his way up until he rooked his way into the bank president's job, the past President had been hiding booze in the vault during the Probation Era until good old Sammy boy caught him and turned him in.

Sammy, as he hated to be called, was devoutly against the consumption of anything that contained alcohol, or so that was the front he put up. In truth, the old man was a boozer and a philanderer. Many were the times he had been seen sneaking out of Marla Cross, his head teller's back door in the middle of the night, chuckling to himself and drunk as a skunk. Hell, his old lady had me follow him a year back and after the report I gave her she lowered the boom on him, told him she didn't want a divorce, of which he would have never given her, but wanted him to pay her a very good stipend to the tune of one thousand dollars a month or she would tell the whole city what a reprobate he was. Needless to say Mrs. Barker is living high on the hog; the new Packard sitting in their driveway proves it. Still, Sammy hasn't changed, he and Marla getting it on three times a week, undercover of course or so he thinks.

I stopped by the bank to see Sammy before I went back to the office, Sammy his usual self as he walked over to see what I wanted. I asked if Bruce Stedman worked here and he crossed his arms and rubbed his chin for a moment, the smell of whiskey light on his breath.

"Yes, yes he did," Sammy answered, "He was one of the bookkeepers under my assistant manager Brad. He quit a week ago, why I couldn't tell you. He was a fine bookkeeper and could have gone far here." I cut him off before he started his speech about how banking was a good job for advancement in the world and asked, "Brad here today?" He gave me a smirk and cleared his throat before he spoke again. Old Sammy didn't like to be interrupted.

"No, he is home sick, what is this about?" His face took on a frown as he stood looking at me. I figured he suddenly remembered me and I was gonna get nowhere in a few seconds.

"Bruce Stedman was murdered so I wanted to ask some questions…" he cut me off with a grunt and shook his head.

"Yes, I read about that in the papers but if you wish to speak to anyone here in the bank about him we will have to contact our lawyers first. Good day *Mr.* Black." He arched one eyebrow and one hand came up and twirled the end of his mustache as a smile crossed his face. Yeah, he had recognized me.

I chuckled as he walked away and I headed toward the door. Yeah, he had made me once his rummy eyes cleared and he got a good look at me. As for contacting the bank's lawyers, well, the old man's brother was one of the bank's lawyers and he hated my ass as much as Sammy did, claimed I had besmirched his the name, that Sammy was a pillar of strength in the community, to which I replied, 'only in the bedroom, buddy, only in the bedroom'.

****

I hustled back to the office to see Shelly and fill her in on what I was doing, the girl glad to see me. When I stepped in the door she stood and in three steps had her arms around me laying a lip lock on me that took *my* breath away.

"I missed you," she whispered in my ear as she hugged me.

"I can see that." I hugged her back. In the three years we have been together I still can't get enough of her. She is quite a woman my Shelly. One day we plan to get married but for right now we're just playing it by ear, me waiting for her to set a date and also waiting until I'm not too big of a risk to her. That, meaning it could be a long time from now before we tie the knot but she seems to be willing to wait as she told me once, "You've already sampled the milk so why worry about buying the cow."

I told her what had happened since I last saw her. She nodded as she walked around her desk, picked a notebook from the top and flipped it open.

"I went down to Benny's for a cup of coffee while you were gone and Stella and I had a little chat. She told me about this guy who came in asking about you. He wanted to know where your office was and if you were in. Stella's a smart cookie so she told him she wasn't for sure when you came in, he'd just have to drop by and check." Shelly flipped through her notes, tapped the eraser end of the pencil on her front teeth before she spoke. "She described him as skinny but not the weak kind of skinny. He talked with a slight accent but the one thing that made her shiver was the scar on his face and his eyes. The scar she said was nasty looking. It seemed to glow but his eyes were dark, sinister, made chills run up her back."

"Sounds like Freddy," I nodded.

"She said he had on gloves, the kidskin kind like you buy in the men's shops. She also told me he didn't take them off even when he ate." Shelly closed the notebook and did a curtsy. Yes, she can be a little smartass at times but I love her for it. It makes life interesting between us. I stepped over and gave her a kiss on the cheek as I headed back toward the door and spoke.

"Okay, now here's what I want you to do. I'm gonna go talk to Fisk so when I leave, put your artillery on and if Striker's face even peeks in the door put a bullet in it."

"Gotcha." I gave her a nod and stepped out the door onto the sidewalk, the sun dipping down in the west. Only half of it showed above the buildings and the temperature was dropping. I tightened the belt on my trench coat and shoved my hands in my pockets. I heard the sound of Shelly locking the door loud in the almost deserted street as I headed toward Kelso's to have a little talk with Fisk.

****

The usual crowd was present at Kelso's with a few Army and Marines mixed in, the soiled doves chatting them up to buy drinks. The boys were lapping up the booze, laughing and talking; some even had an arm tossed around some of the girls and if they bedded them down they would sure regret it in a few months, a visit to the army sawbones required. I waved at Kelso and headed toward Fisk's office, last booth on the west side of the building.

Kelso was watching a couple of Army boys who were getting loud about the middle of the bar, arguing about how many Germans they were gonna kill once they got across the pond and it looked as if the argument might get physical. If I were those two I would take it outside before I threw a fist because Kelso would end it before it started.

Kelso is a tall broad shouldered man with thick arms, knuckle scared hands that when they get hold of you, you *know* you have been gotten hold of. He has a rugged face, square chin and a nose that is flat, the nostrils flaring a little. His hair is a little longish and he wears a full beard, trimmed and kept neat. His eyes are what usually stop people from taking an argument too far, dark brown eyes that, when he gets irritated, seem to get darker and smolder. His voice helps also, a deep bass that when he raises it, fills the room which is very seldom. The Equalizer usually comes into play before things get out of hand, a sawed off baseball bat with streaks of red visible in the grain from the past heads he's cracked.

I walked across the floor and slid into the booth with Fisk, his arms folded on top of the table, a beer in front of him. Fisk is another of my information men but unlike Carter, who has the skinny on the inside workings of the gangsters, Fisk has his ear to the beat of the city. If it has happened or is about to happen, Fisk usually has knowledge of it and if he doesn't, he'll find out.

"Sorry to hear about Stedman." He looked up at me, his eyes apologetic.

"Yeah, but if he was up to what I think he was up to he had it coming." I leaned on the table with Fisk and gave a small shrug. Fisk nodded then asked, "So fill me in on what you know?"

I told him what Carter had told me about Stedman's wife pinching the notebook, the two of them trying to blackmail Russo with it.

"Well, you're partly right," Fisk leaned closer as he talked. "They did try to blackmail Russo with the notebook, but he sent a couple of his boys to see if they could get it back by other means. Someone tipped the Stedmans off so they weren't home. Then Biscayne gets wind that Stedman has the book and brings in The Butcher to get her the book because she has the same thing in mind only on a different level. See Max, Biscayne supplied the entertainment when Russo had his parties. The fool kept track of each city favorite plus the girls they slept with." I leaned back in the booth and let out a low whistle.

"So if Biscayne got hold of the book…"

"Very good old buddy," Fisk broke in, "You see, there is a certain name in it of a certain person who has been trying to shut her down for the past year."

"D.A. Brad Wellman?"

"Bingo. This is an election year and if word got out…"

I nodded and knew exactly what he meant. I had heard rumors that Wellman liked catting around but I figured it was just that, rumors. His credentials showed him as a family man, a church goer, a Crusader for the good of the city but that would change if Biscayne got the book. His dirty little secret would be out and his reputation shot. I leaned back on the table again and tapped it with my finger.

"So his crusade to shut her down would either be stopped or she would inform the public of what a reprobate he is."

"Along with about two dozen others in the city that are in high office which means those under her gun will cave to her wiles to keep it all quiet. Wellman is sweating bullets over it. He has contacted a friend of his in the FBI to see if they can do anything about it."

"And?"

Fisk chuckled. "His buddy told him he would talk to his supervisor about it but his best bet was to let Pat and his department handle it. Besides, his buddy told him he had heard you were working the case also."

"I bet that made Wellman feel real good." Wellman and I tolerate each other. The man wished I would bite the dust and I wished he would also which might just happen if Biscayne got the notebook; and if she got the book, he might just do that, but to tell you the truth; I wouldn't wish it on him or any other man in the notebook.

"Any idea where Freddy might be hold up?" I asked Fisk like I'd asked Carter. Fisk shook his head.

"Not yet. He's in the wind for now, but give me a while, I'll see what I can come up with."

I stood, shook Fisk's hand, the fiver in my palm going from mine to his. He nodded and I turned and walked toward the door and caught Kelso out of the corner of my eye, The Equalizer in his hand as he shook it at the two khakis, both of them patting the air with their hands and backing away from the bar.

CHAPTER 5

I turned my coat collar up as I stepped outside to head back to the office. The wind whipped down the corridor of Commercial Street and brought with it a damp coldness which meant that either sleet or snow was headed this way.

As I walked, my mind went back to the Stedman place, the cone shaped piles and the cellar. Striker was meticulous, methodical in his tortures and his searching indicated in the file I had on him. Also, I'm sure Freddy was pissed because he hadn't gotten Monica to fess up where the notebook was or had not located it in his search, which meant he would be looking at other avenues to where it was. Something else bothered me too, the fact that Monica hadn't cracked under the torture. She was pretty cut up and bruised, shredded being more the term.

Which was why I wondered why she had held out. I mean, no notebook is worth that kind of torture especially when she probably knew for certain she was dead even after she told him where it was. Something wasn't right, that something I would have to mull over for a while. I knocked on the door when I reached the office. Shelly pulled back the blind, the muzzle of her .38 showed first.

She smiled and unlocked the door, the .38 still held in a ready position just in case someone was behind me. I chuckled and told her all was clear then asked her if she was hungry? She never said a word, just grabbed her coat and scarf, bundled up, the two of us headed to Benny's.

Benny's, in my opinion, is one of the best eateries in the city, their hamburgers the greatest when he can get the beef. Located by the firehouse, Benny's has been around since the thirties, his daddy opened it just before the depression of which the diner survived. Benny took over five years ago, his daddy dying of a heart attack while he figured out his books in the back office.

Benny is a short fellow, bald headed and chubby cheeked, a salt and pepper mustache under his nose and a double chin that shakes when he laughs along with the rest of him. Tonight he sat at the cash register, a detective magazine in his hands, his mouth slightly moved as he read. He glanced up when we walked in, nodded then went back to reading. I'm sure after he finished what he was reading he would be back to ask me if some of the things written in the magazine had ever happened to me.

We took a table in about the middle of the room, me facing the windows just in case. Stella took our order, a tall blonde that wore her uniform slightly tight to accent the hills and valleys of her form. She and Shelly had worked together when Shelly worked here but that was it. Shelly told me one time she was a cheat who liked to horn in on her station when she got the chance because most people liked setting in Shelly's station, especially the guys. Oh they were friends in a sense, but it was a respectful friendship, which sometimes slipped a little when Stella started to put the moves on me.

Stella handed us a couple of menus, gave me a wink then walked off to give us time to look them over, her hips swayed like a rope bridge as she walked away. Shelly grunted, mumbled under her breath something about a tart as she buried her head back in the menu. I chuckled and closed mine, reached over, cupped my hand under her chin then lifted her head up and smiled.

Five minutes passed and Stella came back, another button on her blouse undone, the smell of her perfume filled the air.

"So what'll you all have?" She smiled at me and gave Shelly a glance.

"A burger with everything." I looked at Shelly and nodded toward Stella.

Stella turned her head and gave Shelly one of those hurry it up looks. Shelly leaned on the table and smiled at Stella, but only with her mouth, Shelly's eyes spitting sparks.

"Yeah, a ham sandwich, trim the fat." Shelly let her eyes drift down to Stella's hips. Stella's mouth dropped open and she started to say something then closed it, her eyes blazing at Shelly. I looked away, mostly to hide the smile on my face.

Stella grunted and walked away. Shelly whacked me on the arm and gave me the look; you guys know the one I'm talking about, the one where you're to blame and not her. I raised my hands and patted the air palms forward and gave her that 'what, me?' look so she whacked me again on the arm, this time a little harder and told me to stop grinning.

She was about to give me another round when Pat came in, nodded at Benny then waltzed over to our table fast. He pulled a chair up, plopped down in it, nodded at Shelly then leaned in close, his voice low as he spoke.

"Got some interesting news for you buddy." He leaned in on the table a little more.

"And that is?" I asked leaning toward him.

"The woman in the Stedman house wasn't Monica, the lab boys found this under the bed when they were going over the room." He reached into his coat pocket and pulled out a photo. In it, two women were posing; silly poses like some women do when they are happy or with a boyfriend. One was Monica Stedman and the other woman looked exactly like her. I showed the picture to Shelly.

"Yeah." Pat took the picture back from Shelly and nodded, "Twins. We checked the finger prints of the dead woman, they belong to her twin sister Mona Farwell. She works at the post office downtown."

I leaned back in my chair and shook my head. Monica's sister had suffered the hell that was meant for her. The beating, the skinning, the shredding of her face all because of some damned notebook a bitch wanted to save her nasty business. The stink of it left a bad taste in my mouth and without knowing it my hands were clenched in fists so tight my fingernails cut groves in my palms. Until now I had just wanted to find Stedman's killer and put him down, now I wanted to put him *and* The Bitch down, put them down hard, make them suffer like Monica's sister had suffered only doing it with lead from a .45.

I jumped when Stella set my hamburger down in front of me, my eyes jumping to hers which made her take a step back, her eyes big as silver dollars as she set Shelly's plate down and took off.

"You okay buddy?" Pat asked. I looked at him and his eyes narrowed. He knew this look, the one that meant a lot of bodies were going to start to pile up before things were done. I pushed my plate back and leaned on the table, my voice low, having a deadly tone to it.

"It wasn't Russo who brought Freddy in." I looked Pat straight in the eye; mine narrowing, "That bitch Biscayne did. She wants the notebook for blackmail reasons."

"I see." Pat stared back at me. I could tell he was waiting for me to continue but I didn't, especially telling him the Stedmans had the same idea and that one of the names in the notebook was Wellman's. After the long pause, Pat stood, shoved the chair in, his eyes still locked with mine.

"You keep me in the loop, and try not to drop too many bodies around."

I nodded. Pat knew just what was going to happen just like it always happened when I decided to put things right, this one going to be put right even if I kept the city morgue hopping until it was over.

****

The burger set heavy on me as Shelly and I walked back to the office, the wind bitterly cold but I barely felt it. Once inside I told her to go on up, I was gonna make sure things were locked down before I came to join her. I checked the doors then sat down at my desk, pulled out my .45 and ejected the clip, pushed the shells out one at a time and let them drop on my desk, counting them, reserving four for Freddy and three for Biscayne.

When the clip was empty, I laid it down and picked up the bullets, opened my desk drawer and took out a switchblade I had confiscated from a punk a few weeks back, the kid having the nerve to try and rob me while I was in the parking lot across from my office where my car was bunked. He tried, but failed, ended up with a broken arm and a busted nose. The cop who took him off my hands told him he was lucky he wasn't dead.

I opened the blade and carved the nose of each lead slug off, flattening out the ends, dum dums they call them. When they went in, they made a small hole, then punched out a fist sized hole when they came out. I smiled and did all seven like that then slid them back in the clip, slammed the clip home and jacked one in the chamber, then let the hammer down on it.

Yeah Freddy, there would be no give yourself up call, just the bark of my .45, the slugs ripping holes out your backside, making you dance the death dance as your lights went out. The same would happen to Biscayne, four slugs with her, the last one going between her eyes.

She deserved no mercy because she gave none, the stories told about her not just stories but truth. She was called "The Bitch" by the girls who worked for her, the woman having a mean streak that wasn't just slapping the girls around, no, she did more than that. Sometimes her girls showed up in the emergency room at City Hospital, their backs slashed, an ear nearly cut off or their face so black and blue they couldn't even see out of their eyes.

That was the worst cases. Most of the time it was broken fingers, smashed toes or broken ribs. Once Ross told me he was filling in one night in the emergency room and one of her girls came in, both hands crushed the tread marks of the tires still on the backs of her hands. Ross told me he had tried to get the girl to stay the night in the hospital, to tell him who had done this to her but she refused. The goon who came in later growled at him to fix her up so they could get the hell out of there. Ross did, but he didn't like it.

I grinned and shoved my .45 home, stood and walked out to the stairway which lead up to the apartment, the sound of the radio drifting down to me, Shelly humming to the music as I stepped into the apartment, closed the door, took her in my arms and hugged her close and hard till the hate and anger faded away.

But sleep wouldn't come this night so I sat up and mulled over things in my head about the case, the ashtray next to my easy chair filled with cigar butts. I wondered why Mona was there in Stedman's house. It was possible that Monica had sent her to gather a few things to bring to her where she was hid out and Freddy had caught her, mistaken her for Monica and did his dirty deed. I needed to go back to see if there was anything that would give me an idea where Monica might be, something the lab boys had missed, that gnawing in my brain getting stronger and keeping me awake until the sun peeked into the windows.

Shelly woke and made coffee, kissed me on the cheek but didn't ask why I hadn't come to bed last night. She knew that on cases like this I sometimes chased the sandman away to keep focused, which didn't do me any good, my temperament getting pretty nasty until the job was done. I drank a cup of Joe then kissed Shelly on the forehead, told her I would be back in a few which meant I might show up late or not at all, crossed the street, crawled in and cranked over my car, the old girl growled slow for a couple of turns then fired up. I let her run for a few minutes to get her juices flowing then pulled out onto the street toward Stedman's house, the gnawing getting stronger.

CHAPTER 6

The house looked the same as the last time I was here, a one story faded white clapboard structure with green shutters, one on the front hanging by a hinge. I crawled out and walked up to the door, looked over the seal Pat's boys had put on the door and noticed it had been broken. I slid my .45 out and cocked it, nudged the door with my finger, the door opening slightly.

I took a deep breath and gave the door a shove, the glass in it rattling as it hit something behind it. I slid through in a crouch, swept the room and listened. After a few minutes I moved toward the kitchen, pushed the door open easy, looked through the crack and saw nothing. I checked the rest of the house, the rooms all empty.

I went into the bedroom and looked it over again, scanned the floor, the walls, and the furniture. I stepped over to the closet and opened the door, the hangers still there, the dresses that had hung on them which had been slashed to shreds taken for evidence. There were a few pairs of shoes there also, the insides pulled out and tossed on the floor.

There was a light in the closet so I pulled the chain; a bulb lit the dark corners, a suitcase sat in the right corner, a clean spot where another one had sat beside it looked up at me, dust outlined the clean spot.

I stood and turned, looked at the room again, thought back as to how it looked before. Most of it was the same except the suitcase missing, a dresser drawer open, and some cedar chips lying on the floor in front of it. There had also been a jewelry box on top of the dresser which wasn't there now. I looked down beside the dresser and saw it, lying in the floor, empty as my pockets.

I picked it up and looked it over, nothing but a cheap cufflink and tie tack in the floor underneath it. I closed the jewelry box and sat it back on top of the dresser, shaking my head. My bet was Monica had waited until the cops had taken off, gave it another day then came back for what clothes had survived and her jewels to pawn for some quick getaway money. I walked back out into the main room and picked up the phone, calling Pat and asked if they had cataloged everything in the bedroom. Pat said yeah so I asked for a list. He asked why so I told him I'd fill him in later then hung up, Pat still talking into the other end of the receiver.

I took one last look into the bedroom and grunted, most of the piles had been cleaned up the lab boys taking some of the stuff to get prints off the rest left lying. They had even dusted the door frames going into the bedroom; black smudges dotted the white wood work. I turned and walked toward the bedroom doorway, clamped down hard on the cigar in my mouth, cursed them for not pulling the sheets off the bed before the news hawks had flashed their pictures, their flash bulbs lying on the floor around the bed where they had popped them out.

The only picture that had made the papers was a shot of the house. Avery Sikes, the editor kept the others in check probably because Pat had told him to or he would be on his ass. I walked back out in the living room and stood for a moment. There was something I was missing, something that the gnawing told me was right in front of me. I went toward the doorway then to the front door, the gnawing snickering and eating away at the edges of my mind.

I cussed and went out. I hated it when the little bastard did that to me, stayed just out of sight until he wanted to let me know where I had screwed up, then shrieked with laughter once what he had hid came to light. I walked back to the car, crawled in and went to see Pat for the list.

****

I stopped by the Station and picked up the list of jewels that were in the box. I got it from Gabby, a sweet little clerk that worked on the first floor. Pat had told her to copy the list then when I came in to get it send me up to his office. I winked at her and told her to wait five then call him, tell him I had come in, picked up the list and left before she knew it. She giggled and told me sure, but I would owe her. If I wasn't attached, that owing her would be a pleasurable experience, Gabby a busty blonde with sensuous eyes and enough curves to keep a man busy all night. I winked at her again, took the list, slipped out the door and headed toward Carl Hankins's Pawn Shop over in my part of town.

Carl's Pawn Shop is located one door east of the intersection of Booneville and Commercial Street, right next to the Citizen's Drugstore on the corner. He used to be located across the street on the west side of the fire station but the offices upstairs or should I say the wire service caught fire and nearly burned the building to the ground. Of course he knew nothing about that and Pat couldn't tie him into it so he walked. But that doesn't mean he wasn't innocent, I mean I know this street and let me tell you, Carl wasn't any angel. Carl's business suffered a lot of smoke and water damage but he had insurance so it wasn't a total lose.

You can pawn almost anything at Carl's as long as it isn't stolen and if he finds out it is he doesn't deal with you anymore plus he turns you in to the cops since they've had their eye on him since the fire. Carl's biggest item to deal in is musical instruments, mostly in guitars which was what he and a young fellow were arguing about when I walked in.

Carl is a short, stocky fellow with a bald head, a round face, bushy eye brows and a double chin. He always dresses in a suit but the minute he gets to work, he shucks the jacket, rolls up his sleeves and loosens his tie. The kid was tall, a pompadour haircut, leather jacket and blue jeans, his flannel shirt a little thin in fabric, and his jeans a little faded in color.

I nodded at Carl when he looked at me then I leaned against the counter, pulled out a cigar and lit up as Carl argued with the kid over the price of a guitar.

"Look kid." Carl crossed his arms over his chest as he spoke. "Fifty is the lowest I can go for a guitar like this, I mean, the damned thing is almost perfect."

"Well I only got twenty-five," the kid said in almost a whisper, his eyes caressing the guitar. "And I got an audition at KWTO in an hour."

"Is that so, what happened to the guitar you were going to use?" Carl asked.

"Had to sell it to get to Springfield. I figured I could get one for less than what you want." The kid looked at him smiling.

"You any good?" Carl asked.

"Passable." The kid shrugged.

"Tell you what I'm gonna do. You play something for me and if you're any good, I'll sell it to you for twenty-five." Carl grinned then winked at me.

The kid picked up the guitar, strummed it, tweaked a couple of strings to his satisfaction then started to play. As I live and breathe, if I hadn't grabbed the cigar from my mouth it would have hit the floor. He played Wildwood Flower, his fingers flying over the strings, each note loud and clear as he picked out the tune. When he was done, both of us just stood there then Carl started to clap, chuckled as he nodded at the kid.

"Well, what do ya think Max?" He looked at me and jerked a thumb at the kid.

"If you don't sell it to him, I'll buy it for him."

"You heard the man. Where's my money?" Carl held his hand out.

The kid gave us a big grin, handed over the money, re-cased the guitar, locked it down and headed toward the door. I walked over to Carl and shook my head, Carl shaking my hand as I leaned on the counter in front of him.

"That kid got a name?" I asked him.

"Hayworth, he said he's from Gainesville, damn he was good." Carl placed both hands on the counter and leaned toward me. "So what brings you into my humble abode?"

"Jewelry." I said.

"Well, gonna buy that little filly of yours a better ring than what you gave her?" he asked. I shook my head no and pulled out the list.

"The one I got her she likes just fine." I handed him the list. "This jewelry would have been pawned by a red headed woman and she might have been in a hurry."

"Is that so?" Carl took the list, walked over to the case where he kept all of what he called 'his finest'. Most of the stuff in the case was cheap, only a few of the rocks were of any value. He checked the list then the case, his eyes roved over the stuff in the case then back to the list.

"Nope, nothing here that is on the list, but that don't mean she didn't come in and try to pawn the stuff." Carl handed back the list. "Eddie was here yesterday while I took a day off; he might have seen her and looked at the stuff."

"Is he around?" I shoved the paper back in my trench coat pocket.

"He went to lunch, but when he comes in I'll ask him and get back to you, and I'll call the other guys. I ain't the only pawn shop in town, maybe the best, but not the only one."

I chuckled, thanked him and walked toward the door and out, the wind having picked up, clouds having rolled in, the skies graying. There was a wet bite in the air, a flake or two drifting down around me. From the looks of things it would be snowing in another hour. January in the Ozarks, ya gotta love it.

I was halfway back to the office when Pat rolled up, slid into the curb and motioned for me to get in. I opened the passenger door and crawled in, the car warm, Pat's face even warmer.

"What the hell you mean ducking me?" He glared at me.

"Whatever do you mean?" I said in mock surprise.

"Damn it." Pat shook his head. "Milt Folks said he saw you talking to Gabby after she told me you had gotten away before she could call. I confronted her about it and she told me not to call her a liar or she would get her brother to visit me. He works patrol and is as big as a house."

I laughed. Gabby's brother Danny WAS big, but not by house standards. The guy was just huge. His partner, Bill Hoteling, told me one time he and Danny had gotten a call up on South Street, a bar fight to which they answered. He said Danny waded in and when all was said and done, the paddy wagon was full and Danny didn't have a scratch on him although a few of the bar patrons suffered various lumps on their heads and black eyes.

I told Pat not to worry, nothing was going to happen

and he grunted, telling me I better hope to hell I was right. I shook my head and patted him on the shoulder then asked, "Did you have a watch on the house after your boys finished up?"

"Well, we're a little shorthanded," he growled at me, that 'because of the war' look on his face. "The best I could do was have a patrol go by and check every so often, why?"

"Someone went in between patrols. They took a suitcase and cleaned out one of the dresser drawers. How come the jewels weren't brought back to the Station?"

"They were fakes, paste."

"Who told you that?"

"Bill Case. He works part time for old man Smyth the rock cutter. He's been learning the trade because he said it paid more than snapping photos of dead people. The only things in the dresser drawers were a few underthings that had been ripped up."

Which weren't there on my last visit.

I nodded and thought back to the drawer, remembering it in my mind, wondering why someone would want ripped up skivvies. Then I grinned and asked Pat if he was done. He grunted he was then warned me to keep him posted. I told him I would and he mumbled something about hell freezing over as I crawled out of the car, walked the rest of the way to the office. Sleet started to fall with a few snowflakes mixed in as I stepped inside.

CHAPTER 7

Sometimes things are right in front of a person's nose and they don't see them. This was one of those times. The ripped up undies that had been taken had been a ruse to throw us off. I suspected the real reason the drawer was empty was because it had been taken out and something taken from the underside of it then put back in.

I went back to the house, the door closed this time and locked. I pulled out a set of keys and opened the door with a skeleton key, pushed it open, stepped inside and went to the bedroom. I moved the dresser and found the undies stuffed behind it, most of them in tatters. I tossed them on the floor, took the dresser drawer out, flipped it over and grunted. What I thought might be taped to the bottom of the drawer was not there. I tossed the drawer on the bed and leaned on the dresser for a second, the jewelry box sitting in a different place from where I had put it on my last visit.

I picked it up and inspected it again, the inside lined with felt, one end of the box looking funny. I remembered one time my Aunt Millie had a jewelry box that had a hidden bottom in it, she used to keep her valuables in the hidden compartment. I chuckled and took out my pocket knife, opened it and stuck the blade in one end and levered up. The bottom popped loose and a hidden compartment stared me in the face. The box wasn't big enough to hold a notebook but it was big enough to hold a key, maybe a key to something in the cellar and I had an idea what that something was.

I set the jewelry box back on the dresser and walked out into the main room, looked over the mess that was still on the floor and noticed pieces of the trash having been kicked out of the way. The two angels were gone. I followed the trail and it took me to the kitchen, the cellar door ajar.

I swung it open and hit the light switch at the top of the stairs, another set of footprints going down, these smaller than my number nines. At the bottom of the stairs I stopped, the wardrobe cabinet had been opened, a metal box lying on the floor in front of it. I kicked it over so I could see inside, knowing full well that it was empty but it wasn't. Lying in the dirt was a tag, a scrawl of handwriting on it. I was about to kneel down and give it the once over when dust from the floor above trickled down on me.

I shoved the tag in my coat pocket as my other hand dipped under my coat and pulled out my .45 and cocked the hammer as I stepped back into the darkness of the cellar. I watched the steps and waited. Whoever it was, was good, their footsteps so soft I could hardly hear them. They stopped at the doorway, a shadow fell across the steps from the light coming out of the kitchen. I heard a match strike then the sizzle of a fuse.

"Shit!" I hissed between my teeth as I watched a stick of dynamite bounce down the steps then fall between them. I bolted for the cellar doors, hit them hard but they didn't budge. I fired my .45 where I thought the lock might be then hit the doors again just as the stick of dynamite went off, the force of the explosion slammed me into the doors and through them.

I hit the ground hard; my ears rang as the world went in and out of focus. I pushed myself to my feet and stood, staggered a few feet then hit the ground again as debris fell around me, a black curtain engulfed over me as the world fell away behind it.

****

Shelly was the first one through the door of the emergency room, the nurse that tried to stop her from coming back to where I was almost getting a black eye. Ross stopped her before she could and led her back to where I sat on a table; the other doctor, Rains putting the finishing touches on the bandage that decorated my arm.

I had a hell of a headache, my ears still rang a little but all in all I was lucky. My slugs had torn the wood around the lock enough that when the dynamite went off, the doors gave and I went flying out which was all that saved me from being killed. I came out of it pretty good considering, just a concussion and a cut arm, the wood from the door ripped a gash in it when I was blown from the cellar.

Shelly stood by until the Doc was done, her eyes drilled me then softened when she came to me and hugged me, just missing the stitched up arm. I got dressed with Shelly's help and stepped out into the waiting room where Pat stood that 'I outta kick your ass' look on his face.

"Okay hotshot," he growled, "what happened?"

"Besides someone trying to kill me?" I grinned.

"Damn it Max," he started to say and I held up my hand to stop him.

"Let's go to my office, I'll fill you in there." I motioned toward the doorway. He grunted and followed Shelly and me out to my car that had a cracked windshield plus a dented fender, Pat telling me part of the house had fell on it. I groaned as Shelly led me to the passenger side, me complaining to her I had already had a brush with death and didn't need another, her driving skills having a lot to be desired.

****

"Now, I ask again, what happened?" Pat spoke as I settled into my chair behind my desk and fished around in the drawers for a bottle of aspirin, the pain killer they had given me in the emergency room beginning to wear off. My arm was giving me fits and my head was also.

"We should have looked the house over better." I found the bottle of aspirin, unscrewed the cap and shook four into my hand, popped them into my mouth and chewed. "Someone stuffed the undies behind the dresser to throw us off in case we came back. I also found a false bottom in the jewelry box. It held a key to the wardrobe in the cellar which wasn't open the first time I went down there."

"So what was in the wardrobe?" Pat tipped his fedora onto the back of his head.

"A metal box."

"And in the box?"

I shrugged and his face went red. He knew I was holding back but he also knew if he pressured me he would only get another shrug. He leaned forward in his chair, his eyes narrowed and his face got redder, his voice tense as he spoke.

"The D.A. wanted me to pull you in for questioning. I told him it would do no good because if he tried to force you to talk he would only get the run around like I am now. I told him I would handle it and he told me I'd better, so give!"

I shook my head at him. "Just tell him I have a thin lead, real thin, let him chew on it."

"More like he will chew on me, so how thin is this

lead?"

"So thin it's almost transparent."

"Damn!" Pat cussed. I hated lying to him but in truth it was a thin lead but more opaque that transparent. I just needed to talk with some people who could clue me in. He shook his head as he leaned forward in his chair, his eyes locked with mine.

"I'm sure your picture will be in the papers," he growled at me, changing the subject and smirking. "Barney Rutherford snapped it while they loaded you in the ambulance, then his buddy Collin wanted to know if you were dead or alive."

"And you told them?"

"I told them you were slightly out of it but alive. Then they wanted to know if you were the one who caused the explosion. I gave them the standard no comment but would make a full statement to the press once we found out what happened." Pat sat back glared at me. "So were you the cause?"

"No, someone else, and before you get nasty, I never saw them, just heard them on the floor above me. I suspect it was some of Russo's boys. They've probably been watching the house off and on and spotted my car in the driveway so they decided to solve two problems in one, kill me in the explosion and the fire would destroy the book."

Pat thought for a moment then looked at me and nodded but before he could ask why they hadn't searched for me in case I had escaped I asked, "Your boys located Monica yet?"

"Nada, she's in the wind. We even talked to her brother-in-law and he told us he hadn't seen her in over a month."

I closed my eyes and nodded, the dull pounding in my head had escalated to the boom of a bass drum. I grabbed the aspirin bottle again, shook two more out and chewed them up.

"How can you do that?" He made a face and shivered.

"They work faster if you chew them up dry." Which was a lie but he didn't know that. I just did it because it makes his face screw up when I do it.

"You mind if I have a talk with her brother-in-law?" I recapped the bottle as I leaned back in my chair and rubbed my temples.

"Knock yourself out." Pat waved his hand in the air. "You're probably going to anyway. Just let me know if you get anything out of him we couldn't. Be nice about it okay? I don't want Wellman crawling all over my ass because you didn't play nice."

"Now why would I not play nice?" I gave him a big grin.

"Just keep me in the loop," Pat growled, pointing a finger at me as he stood and walked to the door and out, muttered a goodbye to Shelly as he left and slammed the door on his way out. Pat and I go back a ways, the first case we worked being a counterfeit and human trafficking case. He knew how I worked; he also knew how I could get people to talk when I wanted them to. No hitting or threatening to blow their brains out, though I must admit on some people it does work. No, I just ask questions, most of those questions asked with a nasty smile on my lips and venom in my voice. Crazy eyes help also.

I reached for the aspirin bottle again just as Shelly came into my office, a newspaper in her hands. The bass drum was beating louder and harder but before I could unscrew the top off the bottle, Shelly snagged it from me, tossing the paper on the desk in front of me.

"How many you had?" She shook the bottle at me.

"Not enough." I gave her a pitiful look. "My head feels like a bass drum is pounding inside of it."

"How many?" she asked again. This time it was her mothering voice, stern and ready to pounce if she thought I was lying. You don't want her to pounce, not in any shape or form because her tongue is barbed. When she does it lashes the flesh until you tell the truth. At least that's what she does to me when she catches me in an untruth.

"Six," I let out a sigh.

"No more." She glared at me. "They'll kick in in a bit. Have you seen the evening edition?"

She pointed at the paper, a slight smile on her face. I picked up the paper and opened it to the front page, the headline reading;

"Maverick detective Max Black found outside blown up house,
Is more to come?"

Under the headline was a picture of the ambulance attendants loading me onto their buggy, another picture beside it of the house, nothing but a mass of burning rubble. The squib was written by old buddy Barney Collins, one of the reporters who had deemed me a city menace, a man of the past who used Wild West tactics to solve my cases. Shoot first ask questions later he had once printed in one of his squibs about me. So to piss him off farther, I had some business cards printed up as a joke and sent him one, thanking him for my motto. Art Rowen, The Daily News' editor told me Barney took it as an insult and swore he would run me out of business. Art told him to knock it off, that I had helped bring down a lot of bad guys and if he couldn't take a joke he better not dish anything out that would come back on him and bite him in the ass.

I tossed the paper on my desk and rubbed my face, the aspirins were kicking in but not enough, the drum was dimmer but hadn't stopped. Suddenly Shelly was behind me, her fingers on my temples gently massaging them as I had done, the drum getting softer and softer. I let out a sigh and leaned back.

"Feel better?" I nodded and relaxed, the drum fading

almost into oblivion.

"What was Pat so pissed about?" she asked still rubbing.

"Something I'm hiding from him." I reached in my jacket pocket and pulled out the tag, lay it on the desk and smoothed it out, the writing a little faded but a number readable.

"I know what that is." Shelly leaned down beside me; her perfume touched my nose, the scent made me think dirty thoughts.

"Okay Watson, what is it?"

"It's a tag for a duplicate key. When I had one made for you for the house the guy wrote my name on it, not a number so he could find it when I went to pick it up." She poked the tag with her finger.

"Pretty good lady." I spun around in my chair, grabbed her and pulled her down on my lap as she giggled. "That a new perfume?"

"Yeah." She slung her arms around my neck. "You like it?"

"Let's go upstairs and I'll let you know." I kissed her long and sweet before I turned her loose to head up to the apartment.

CHAPTER 8

Snow, two inches deep played havoc on Commercial Street when I got up the next morning. Already three cars had slid into each other plus two fist fights had broken out because of it. What cops who were on duty had their hands full, one of the mad motorists having slugged a uniform and the wagon wasn't available. It wouldn't start so he had to haul the mad drivers to the Station in his car. I watched this from the window and sipped coffee as I mulled over what I was gonna say to Ralph Farwell when I talked to him.

Acting like a tough guy wouldn't do, I needed to be tactful, try to get him to answer my questions without being an ass which was gonna be hard because that was usually how I got answers from suspects. Of course if he got lippy, then I would do the tough guy routine on him and see where it led.

I walked back into my office, set my cup down on my desk, picked up the tag and looked at it for a few minutes. I wished the damned thing could talk then maybe I could wrap this case up, rap Biscayne in the mouth with the notebook and shut her down, not because she *was* a bitch, but because of the things she had done that the law couldn't prove.

Mary Biscayne owned four houses here in town, one off of South Street just outside the city limits, two in the city but disguised as hotels and one on the north side just outside the city limits just like the south side house. She had been raided numerous times in the city, Pat and his boys closing her down for a while but she always opened back up. As of late someone had been warning her when there was going to be a raid so when Pat got there, nothing but residents and hotel staff was present, no johns to bust her and close her down.

I stuck the tag in my pocket, thinking of places where Monica might have had the key made. My first place to check would be Mason's Hardware store down the street. Old Mason was a good friend and even though he was close to seventy, his mind was sharp as a tack. If he made the key he would remember who he had made it for plus what it was for.

I walked behind my desk, taking my .45 rig off the coatrack, sliding it on then took my .45 out of my middle desk drawer, checked the action then slid it home in my rig. My arm hurt a little from last night but I've been hurt worse, a lot worse. Over the years I've been a gumshoe I've been shot, stabbed, beat almost to death now almost blown up. Some have told me I needed to quit playing with the bad boys, but those bad boys are the ones who start the ball rolling. I just finish it.

I took a few steps and walked into the small bathroom I had installed when Shelly came to work for me, just a sink and a stool, Shelly telling me she wasn't going to run up and down the stairs when she needed to piddle. I stood in front of the mirror and fiddled with my tie, pushing it up but not buttoning the collar. If I do it right no one notices anyway. I feel like I'm strangling when my shirt is buttoned tight against my throat.

I combed my hair, black and still full but receding a little. I shrugged and figured someday it would get thin a little at a time then it would be gone. Most of the men in my family had gone bald at one time or the other, my dad lost his rug by the time he was forty. I rubbed my hand over my face and stubble scraped the palm of my hand so I picked up the shaver Shelly had gotten me for my birthday, an electric job that did fine in a hurry, but I still liked the old soap and safety razor the best. Once that was done I splashed on some Old Spice. Someone cleared their throat, me turning toward my kitten. She leaned in the doorway, shook her head and stepped in close, her hands coming up to adjust the tie.

"When are you gonna learn to button the top button of your shirt when you wear a tie?" She fiddled with it, almost got it before it popped back out of the hole again.

"I feel strangled when it's tight like that." I jerked back from her before she tried again.

"I swear Max," she slapped me on the shoulder and grabbed the tie then asked, "Are you gonna be gone all day?"

"Why, you got something planned?" I winked at her.

"Not after last night, no." Shelly smiled an impish smile. "You know, I was thinking; maybe Mason made that key the tag goes to."

"My thinking exactly." I stepped past her and grabbed my jacket off the peg behind my desk. "I'll check him first."

"You do that, and tell his wife I said hi."

I put on my jacket then kissed her on the cheek, grabbed my trench coat off the chair next to the door and shrugged it on. Shelly was walking toward me as I stepped into the doorway to the outer office, then fell backwards, shoving Shelly away from me and the doorway, the sound of a trench gun shattering glass filled the air.

I could feel the heat of the double 00 buck as it passed

over me, some of it hit the brim of my hat and knocked it off. As I hit the floor, my hand came out with my .45. I leaned up a bit, fired at the doorway as my .45 slugs ripped through the air and slammed into the door frame, a couple made him duck.

The trench gun went off again, but this time high and ripped a hole in the wall above my office door, showering plaster down on me. I sat up; ready to fire hoping the hood was still fighting the splinters my slugs had thrown at him and I saw him turning to run. I popped off another shot; this one caught him in the leg. He couldn't quite get out of the doorway. He stumbled then disappeared as I was on my feet and ran toward the doorway, ready to pump out what I had left in the .45.

I heard a car door slam, tires spun on the street, trying to grab the road under the ice. I ducked out onto the sidewalk, tires still spinning, an olive green coup fishtailed on the street, denting the door of a brand new Buick and ripped the chrome off the door. I leaned on the hood of the Buick, pumping two more slugs into the back of coup just as it grabbed pavement and shot forward, weaved again then slid around the corner of the intersection of Booneville and Commercial to disappear.

Shelly peeked around at me; her .38 gripped in her hand, her face a little pale.

"Are they gone?" Her voice was shaky.

"Yeah kitten, all gone." I ejected the clip from my .45 and shoved in another. I looked down; drops of blood spattered the ice and snow on the sidewalk leading out to the street.

"At least I hit the bastard." I looked back at her and pointed to the trail in the snow. I followed it, the trail ended in a bright red spot where the car had been. I shoved my pistola home and walked back to Shelly. She had gone back in and picked up my fedora, the brim partly ripped away from the front of the hat. I took it from her, her eyes big and round as I looked it over.

"Damn." I looked at her. "I liked that hat!"

****

Pat sat in my office, me telling him the details of the gun fight, him taking notes. His lab boys processed the scene, what there was of it to process, mostly just blood in the snow and footprints. Really nothing to go on but it was evidence. What few people were on the street were being questioned by the uniforms. They got four different descriptions, each one ranging from low life hood to the devil himself. Shelly called the Ennis Brothers and asked if they could come down to do something with the door. They had told her yeah, but it might be later in the evening until I took the phone from her and told them to get their skinny asses down here or I would tell Pat about their still. Ten minutes later they were on the scene.

"Somebody wants you out of the way." Pat flipped his notebook shut and stowed it in his pocket.

"Yeah." I leaned on my desk, pointed to my hat lying on top of it. "Looks like dead out of the way."

"Dead to get whatever you've got." Pat shook a Lucky from his deck and lit up.

"What makes you say that?" I gave him a puzzled look like I didn't know what the hell he was talking about.

"Oh Hell Max." Pat blew smoke, his face tense. "You know they think you have the notebook."

"What about you, do you think I have it?" I watched him. He drew in another deep drag and let it out slow before he answered.

"No, but I think you might know where it is."

"Well, let's put it this way, what they think I know will make them careless."

"Which is exactly the way you want it."

I nodded and a smile crossed my face. "Especially

Biscayne and her hired maniac."

Pat grunted as he leaned forward and flipped ash into my ashtray.

"Look Max, if you know where this damned notebook is why not let me in on it?"

I shook my head. "Not this time old buddy, you work your angles I'll work mine."

"You know I could haul your ass downtown for suppressing evidence?"

"What evidence, all I have is hearsay that doesn't fall in the realm of evidence, like I said…"

"Yeah, yeah." Pat stood grinding out his cigarette in the ashtray. "You just watch your ass you hear me."

"Why Pat, I didn't know you cared." I chuckled. Pat grunted, turned and stalked out of my office like he did the last time, pissed and growling at the Ennis Brothers to get the hell out of his way. I leaned back in my chair and pulled the tag from my pocket, then slid it back in again. I hated lying to him but like I said, I had nothing more than hearsay and a piece of paper to work with. The tag might not be what I thought it was which that would put me back to square one.

Besides, with the murder of Mona it had become personal. Nobody should have to suffer like that just because a bitch wanted a notebook to keep her in business and the D.A. under her thumb. Anytime they were about to close in on her for anything, she would waive the notebook in his face and he would either take care of it or have his name plastered all over the newspapers. Really, it served him right but that wasn't my concern. Hell, I'd love to see the little bastard squirm, but I wanted Freddy and this was the only way to get him.

I mean, two people have died, one because Stedman thought he could possibly squeeze a few thousand out of Russo with the damned book and another because she didn't know anything which Freddy thought she did. My mind went through a scene of him questioning her, his face twisted up in a lunatic's grin, asking with each slice of the knife where the book was, her telling him she didn't know. I cursed and shut those images out. Freddy was gonna die and die nasty once I found him but I'd have to have the notebook to do it.

I stood and glanced at the clock, the time just after noon so I grabbed my trench coat and pulled it on, stepped out into the outer office and out the front door.

CHAPTER 9

Mason's Hardware was four doors down from my office. Most of Pat's crew had finished up and the few stragglers that hung around were looking for somewhere to get warm. Even the reporters who usually hung around until the last dog was dead had taken off. I stepped up into the doorway of Mason's and pushed the door open, a bell jingled to let them know they had a customer. Mason had opened the store around 1919, him and Josie having come down here from Chicago to get away from the big city plus open a business of his own.

Mason had everything a fellow could want to fix whatever from nuts and bolts to bathroom fixtures *if* you had an indoor water closet. I walked down the center aisle toward the main counter, Josie stood behind it, checking over some product as she scribbled on a clipboard.

Josie is a small woman, by small I mean she stands just a little over 4'6", her dress old fashioned and covered her from the neck down to her ankles but you could still see that even at her age, she was still a shapely woman, the wool of her dress hugged the curves just right. Her hair was gray, put up in a tight bun, her nose small, graceful, her lips pushed in and out as she went over the sheet on the clipboard, every once in a while letting out a raspberry sound.

She looked up as I walked toward her, her blue eyes slightly magnified behind the wire rimmed glasses she wore. She lay the clipboard down and smiled her teeth white and even in her mouth.

"You come to see Mason, no?" she asked, her voice had a slight accent to it.

"Is he in?" I asked.

"He's in the workshop trying to make the radio work. It went out last night right in the middle of Amos and Andy. My word did he throw a fit." She chuckled, "I tell him to just get another one but he gives me the same spiel about costing too much money."

I laughed. Mason was a tightwad of the worst kind. Josie once told some of her friends he still had the first dollar he had ever made.

"Go on back. Just watch out for flying tools." She waved me behind the counter and I walked around toward the curtained doorway into the back of the hardware store to what Mason calls the workroom, more like a storeroom with a few worktables for small jobs Mason sometimes took on. He was huddled over one, the innards of his radio in front of him, in one hand a tube, the other wiggled the tubes in the radio and muttered curses came from his lips.

I leaned up against the table next to him, watched him for a few minutes until he glanced at me and asked, "What's on your mind Max?"

"A key." I pulled the tag out of my pocket and shoved it under his nose. "Did you make one for this tag number?"

"Let me see." He tossed the tube on the table taking the tag. "Yes, I do believe this is one of mine."

He walked over to a desk by the curtained door, sat down and took out a metal box, flipped it open to go through its contents. After a few minutes he pulled out a card and nodded.

"Ja." He handed me the card. "Two months ago a redheaded woman she came in, wanted this key made."

"Did she have a name?" I asked.

"No, she never said, just wanted the key made and left a phone number for me to contact her when it was done." His shoulders rose and fell in a shrug.

"Was it a duplicate?"

"Ja, she wanted to know if I could make it from a clay impression. She said it was to a lockbox that her husband had the only key to. She said she wanted to see what he was hiding and told me she would make it worth my while so…"

He shrugged and gave me a lopsided smile. I mean, I couldn't blame him, times were hard and he wouldn't know if she was telling the truth or not, which she was not.

"She was a redhead you say?"

"Ja." His lopsided smile grew and he winked. "She was well built and smelled wonderful."

"No name or address huh?" I asked again.

"No, no name, she told me she would be back in a few days to see if I was done making the key and left but I did hear her tell the taxi driver an address when I followed her out to go get some lunch at Benny's."

I smiled as Mason wrote it down on a piece of paper, handed it to me and winked. I nodded, thanked him and headed toward the front door.

****

The address was for the Colonial Hotel, no room number, just the address. I snagged a cab and told him to take me there, the driver nodded and asked if I wanted to get there fast or alive. I told him alive.

"The streets pretty rough huh?" I leaned back in the

seat as he pulled out and slid a little on the street.

"Yeah, especially around the square, the damned city ain't doing such a good job this year." He shrugged his shoulders. "The war and all ya know?"

"Yeah." I then decided to take a chance and ask, "Listen, you wouldn't happen to have picked up a redheaded gal a few weeks back, took her to the Colonial Hotel?"

"A redheaded dame, yeah, I picked up a redhead in front of Mason's bout three weeks ago." He glanced at me in the rearview. "She was a looker let me tell you, stacked and had on this perfume that smelled out of this world."

"So I've been told," I chuckled.

"Yeah, my old lady was to wear something like that I'd stay home more," he grinned at me in the rearview mirror, "She was real jumpy though, every car that passed us she kinda slumped down in the seat 'till they passed. She acted like she was in trouble."

He was still looking at me in the rearview, his eyes waiting for an answer. I just shrugged and said nothing. The driver watched me for a moment and when I still didn't answer his eyes went back to the road. It took us fifteen minutes to get to the hotel; his route took us through the square and down St. Louis Street where he slid into the curb and stopped just short of the ass end of a Packard. I crawled out, paid the man then walked down the sidewalk to Jefferson and the entrance of the hotel.

As I rounded the corner, I glanced north down Jefferson Street and shook my head. A few cars had tried to make the slick hill but failed some still halfway out in the street, the rest still at the bottom of the hill parked wherever they could find a spot. The cars abandoned on the hill had tickets on them, illegal parking, I figured the courthouse would be a buzz with angry motorist demanding the tickets be dismissed.

There were a few people coming in and out of the

hotel, mostly salesmen carrying sample cases, one almost busted his ass as he walked south on Jefferson, his sample case the only thing that saved him when he went down, the case slammed onto the sidewalk, the salesman sitting down on it. He yelped then stood real quick, looked around to see if anyone had seen him then picked up the case and walked away, rubbing his right ass cheek as he went.

I chuckled and stepped inside the hotel, the entryway warm enough to make me unbutton my coat and undo my scarf. The main lobby was busy, people sat around in the front lounge drinking coffee and reading the local papers. A big fireplace was going strong, one of the bell boys poking at it with a poker getting ready to toss another log on.

Usually there are three people around the front desk, two girls and the manager of this joint, his office just to the left behind the desk. Today there was only one girl on duty, a tall blonde in a tight skirt and sweater, hustling around waiting on customers. I leaned on the desk and pulled out a cigar, lit up and waited for her to finish with a fellow who argued with her over his bill.

"This is outrageous." He thumped the bill with his finger. "I was assured that this was a single room, I'm not paying for a double!"

"Well, it was a single until your wife called down and ordered extra towels this morning," the blonde said, the corners of her mouth turned up slightly.

"My w-wife?" The man stuttered, his face going red.

"Yes sir or she claimed to be," the blonde answered, her smile growing.

I snickered and the guy shot me a look so I shrugged. The Colonial wasn't like the Missouri Hotel, You rent a single here and it was a single until you were caught with someone sharing the room, wife or not, then they upped the rates.

"Uh, well, maybe we could cut a deal here." He winked at her.

"And maybe you could just pay the bill," a voice growled as it walked past me. Dell Decker is a tall, broad shoulder man dressed in a tailored suit and walks with a limp. He used to be a cop until a stray slug in a shootout shattered his knee cap and retired him from the job. Now he works as the Colonial's hotel detective. He looks somewhat like Clark Gable, even sports a mustache like the famous actor and rumor is he stands in front of a mirror pressing the dimple in his chin with his thumb to make it deeper. Dell leaned on the counter as the man's face went redder.

"This is outrageous," the man growled in a low voice. "Yes, I entertained a lady last night but I shouldn't have to pay for her sleeping over!"

"Look at it this way brother." Dell gave him a wicked grin. "You're paying for it twice either way so next time rent a double so this won't happen again."

"Outrageous," the man grunted as he pulled out his wallet and thumbed off a few bills. "And don't expect a tip young lady!"

"Thank you and come again," she said in a sweet voice as she gathered up the money. The man glared at her, grabbed his cases and stomped out the door. I laughed and Dell did also as he came over to where I stood.

"Can you believe it?" He shook his head and jerked a thumb over his shoulder at the guy, "I saw him sneak her in last night before I went off duty, both of them drunk as skunks when they came in. I just hope we don't have to disinfect the room for crabs. So what can I do for you Max?"

"I'm running down a redhead. She was supposed to be berthed here."

"There're a lot of redheads in this hotel. You got a room number?"

I shook my head. "This one was well built but kinda jumpy, like someone was following her. I've also been told she smelled good."

"Yeah, I remember her, tall and built. Lena, you remember her." He turned to the tall blonde, "Is she still checked in?"

"Yeah, I think so." Lena flipped through the register on the desk. She stopped and turned it toward me pointing at the name signed there.

I smiled. "Is she in?"

"I don't know." Lena shook her head. "She is paid for the week so she doesn't turn her key in each time she goes out."

"Is she in trouble?" Dell asked.

I nodded.

"Then let's go see if she's in." Dell bounced off the desk motioned me to follow.

There was a do not disturb sign on room 316's door and after I talked to the maid on this floor, I found out it had been there for a few days. She was going to tell her supervisor about it today if she couldn't get in by knocking. Dell told her not to worry, he would take care of it, pulled out his master key, slid it into the lock and opened the door. The room was a mess, not a lived in mess but a tossed mess. The maid was standing behind us and I heard her say she wasn't cleaning it up as she moved on down the hall.

"Someone was looking for something." Dell's voice was almost a whisper as we looked over the room. I nodded and walked around, surveying things as I did. It was the same as the Stedman place, each section of the room searched, the cast offs piled in a cone shaped pile, couch and chair cushions slit open, the stuffing pulled out, even the backs of the couch and chairs had been slit open. Dell walked over to the phone on the floor and picked it up. It had been taken apart and trashed.

"I'll go downstairs and call the Station." He walked to the door and I nodded but kept scanning the room, taking in everything which was exactly the same as in the Stedman house or at least the main room was. It was the bedroom that was different. From the looks of it, there had been a real knock down drag out in here. Clothes and suitcases were tossed everywhere. A chair was busted like it had been slammed over someone and the bed had been shoved around.

There was also a bottle by the edge of the bed, a whiskey bottle that had been used as a club, broken glass on the bed and floor, the busted upper half sticking out from under the edge of the bed. There was also a trail of blood leading to the window, a smear of blood where someone had opened it. There was also blood on the fire escape and on the outside of the window.

Dell came into the room where I was, his eyes going wide when he saw the blood.

"Is there a body?" His voice was low and his eyes wide.

"No." I walked over to him. "But there was one hell of a fight in here."

"This is not good." Dell shook his head. "Not good at all."

"For them or business?"

"Both," Dell said in a tight voice. "Both."

CHAPTER 10

Pat's boys went over the rooms with a fine tooth comb, photographed, dusted for prints, taking a bloody print from the window plus a couple from the sill. Haralson the manager was pissed, not only at Dell, but at the maid for not checking to see if anyone was in the room. She shot back at him that the do not disturb sign was on the door. He informed her she should have checked anyway.

In the end the maid won the argument. It was hotel policy if the sign was on the door it meant just that, do not disturb. As for Dell, Haralson didn't give him too much grief, Dell being a foot taller than the man and not one to take any shit. Before Pat got there I did my own search of the room, looking for anything that might lead me to Monica. There was nothing.

I was leaning against the wall when Pat and his crew came up; Pat stopped as the boys went in, leaned against the wall with me, his hands shoved in his coat pockets.

"Well?" He gave me a sideways look, his cop eyed stare drilled me.

"Well what?"

"Come on Max, I know you did a search of the room before we got here."

"Yeah, but I found nothing."

"Uh-huh," he grunted.

I grabbed him by the arm and led him down the hallway, a puzzled look on his face as we went. At the end of the hall I pulled the tag out of my pocket and told him what I had learned. Pat looked the tag over then looked me over, a frown crossing his face.

"You should have told me about this." He held the tag up in front of me, "The forensic boys might have gotten some prints off of it."

"Probably all they would have found was Monica's digits on it."

"So why tell me about it now?"

"That fight that took place in the bedroom, I don't think Monica could have done all that damage. Someone else was here with her."

"Freddy?"

"Probably. Whoever it was put up a hell of a fight, my guess is Ralph was with her and Freddy waited till he left slipped into the room and tried to get Monica to talk."

"And Ralph comes back while Freddy is trying to get Monica to tell him where the book is."

I nodded, looked back in the room at the guys sifting through the mess.

"Yeah, and the fight was on. My question is why someone didn't call the desk when they heard the ruckus, especially the way the bedroom looked."

"Maybe the rooms weren't occupied beside this one?" Pat rubbed his chin and bounced off the wall, walking toward one of the room doors and raising his hand to knock, gripping the doorknob and shoving the door open. I saw it coming and I grabbed Pat and pulled him to the floor. There was a loud pop, then a flash and the sound of bits and pieces of metal slamming onto the wall across from the doorway.

"Jesus!" Pat stood up, took his hat off and wiped at the sweat that had broken out on his face, what cops that were in the hall having hit the floor and were now picking their selves up off of it and staring. I stepped over to the door, a couple of uniforms followed me, our pistolas drawn and ready.

Down at the threshold of the door a string lay snapped in two, the smell of cordite strong in the air. A stick, the end shattered, hung down in the doorway, the wood still smoking from the small explosion, a couple of pieces of masking tape still clinging to the charred wood.

Pat was behind me when I stepped in, his eyes looking from the stick to the wall, pieces of metal, nails and shot embedded in the wall.

"How the hell..." He turned to look at me, his thinking mode turned to a puzzled look.

"The string was tied to an eyehook," I said pointing at the bottom of the doorjamb, "then ran to this one then up and tied to the stick where the booby-trap was mounted on the stick. I'd say it was a rubber ball or maybe a small cardboard box filled with gunpowder and shrapnel with a match head for the igniter."

I pointed to the strip of sandpaper with a strike mark on the door frame, a guide kept the stick from being pulled back away from the sandpaper.

"The door is shoved open, breaks the string and then...Boom!"

Pat jumped a little and his eyes jerked up to mine, a hard look crossed his face as he turned and told the officers behind us to check the room on the other side but do it carefully. One of the uniforms nodded and with his buddy went to the other room as we looked around. In a few minutes, one of the uniforms came over and told Pat he needed to come and look, both of us walked over and entered the room, a man lying on the bed, his throat cut from ear to ear, the window open, blood pooled around him on the bed sheets.

He had taken care of business before he had broken into Monica's room, vacated the rooms on either side of Monica's before he started in on her. Dell was in the hall when we came back out, talking with a uniform. Pat and I stepped up to the two of them, the uniform stepped back so we could ask questions.

"Jesus Christ," Dell said as he looked from the blackened doorway to the wall and its jewelry, "What the hell happened?"

Pat ignored him and asked, "This room, who was it rented out to?"

"Some guy by the name of Stall. Lena told me about him and said maybe I should keep an eye on him, he looked creepy." I grunted and told Dell that was an understatement.

"When did he rent the room?" Dell looked at me and I gave a slight shrug as he answered. "Yesterday, the man who was in there had checked out that morning."

I turned and motioned for Pat to follow me into Monica's bedroom.

"No blood in the room so that means he rigged the booby-trap before he came into this room and silenced the guy in the bed." I pointed to the wall on my right and then my left. "Then he breaks in here and snags Monica, or tried to and she fights back, but he subdues her and ties her to the bed."

I walked over to the bed and pointed to the ropes on the headboard and footboard.

"Then he goes out and ransacks the room, hoping maybe the notebook is here and when he sees its not, he goes back in and works her over a little. Enter Ralph…"

"If it was Ralph," Pat cut in.

"Enter Ralph." I shook a finger at him not to interrupt. "By this time Monica has gotten loose from the ropes.

Striker starts after her again, Ralph comes in behind him and the fight is on." I motioned around the room, a couple of uniforms stood behind Pat lapping up my explanation. I grinned and pointed to the whiskey bottle.

"Ralph and Striker are going at it and Monica grabs the whiskey bottle, slams Striker over the head with it, breaks it, but the adrenalin is pumping in Striker and he whirls on her, Monica taking a swipe at him as he comes at her, cutting him before he can grab the broken bottle away. By that time Ralph has a chair and slams it across Striker's back, but still, the adrenalin is pumping, Striker goes down then comes back up, Monica having dropped the bottle, Striker grabbed it and swiped at Ralph cutting him. Monica then grabs a busted leg from the chair and bops Striker on the back of the head and this time knocks him out then Monica and Ralph took a powder out the window."

I took a bow and Pat cussed under his breath. I let a smile grow on my face and walked up to him, patted him on the shoulder as I passed. "Of course this is all hypothetical. You best tell your crew to keep a lid on it though. A few of them might blurt it out if certain reporter's part with enough green and you don't want that do you?"

Pat whirled around and strode past me, catching up with the two who had been listening and gave them the riot act as I walked down the hall past them.

****

To tell you the truth, I was probably right, maybe a few details off here and there but pretty close. I had done this before with Pat, but never with an audience around which was why he was so ticked at me. My guess is the bomb was for me or anyone who decided to check the rooms on either side. Possibly for me, the shit knew my reputation for solving cases and sometimes more, that more being a dead body. The body in the other room was just a warm up for him, like an entrée before the main meal.

The sun had set as I stepped into Kelso's, the wind having died a little and the temperature bottoming out again. Only a few people were there, mostly regulars with a hand full of Army boys quietly discussing which whore house they were going to visit tonight. I walked over to Fisk's office and slid into the seat across from him, a smile on his face as he looked up at me.

"I figured you'd be here sooner or later." He eyed me over the top of the beer in front of him.

"So give me the skinny." I raised my hand and Kelso nodded.

"Well, the word is Freddy got his clock cleaned in a hotel room over on Jefferson Street."

Right so far.

"How well cleaned?"

"Cleaned good. I hear he has a broken wrist and a face that would make his mother flinch if the first one didn't."

Score one for the shamus.

"So who did it?"

"A fellow by the name of Ralph."

"Mona's husband?"

"One and the same. Seems he went to see his sister-in-law a couple of days ago and was followed by Freddy. Freddy checked into the room next door and waited until Ralph left. What Freddy didn't count on was Ralph coming back and the fight was on."

"Yeah, the fight involving a whisky bottle and a chair, how long was Ralph gone?"

"A few hours because when he got back, Freddy had already tied Monica to the bed and did some work on her, nothing drastic, just a little eye opener. Freddy must have left the room for some reason because Monica got loose and waited until he came back, bashing him over the head with the whiskey bottle just as Ralph came back in."

"There was blood on the floor and the fire escape. Any word on who was cut?"

"Both of them. Freddy had the bottle in his hand and was about to work Monica over with it for slamming him over the head. When Ralph came into the room, he took a swipe at him and cut him then Ralph grabbed a chair and took him down then beat him with what was left. I hear Ralph and Monica worked him over pretty good, Ralph cutting him again on the same scar he had with the whiskey bottle before Monica cold cocked him."

Remember what I said? A few minor details? Still, Pat would shit if he heard this.

"What about Russo, he still in the game?" I asked changing horses in midstream.

"Well, yeah, he has men tailing you. I hear he figures you will snag the notebook then he will move in." Fisk jerked his head toward the bar and a guy in khakis and a leather coat, a worn fedora pulled low to hide his face.

"Not to mention Freddy."

"Yeah."

I stood, palmed off the usual fiver to Fisk then started toward the door. I walked up to the bar, shouldered between the hood and a soldier boy, Kelso, who was ready to bring my drink to me, set it on the bar, the guy on the stool trying hard not to make eye contact. I downed the drink then turned the glass over and brought it down hard on the guy's hand on top of the bar, bones crunched and the drink he had taken spewed out of his mouth. The guy next to me gave us some room.

Before he could do anything I grabbed his head and slammed it down on the bar and pinned him there, the Army boys watching in awe as I leaned down close to his head.

"You tell Russo the next one of you goons I see following me I'll put a bullet in their head." I let go of him and walked out the door as the hood dropped to the floor, the soldier boys talking in a low whisper as Kelso walked around to him, grabbed the hood by the coat and escorted him to the side door of his establishment, then tossed his ass out in the alley.

****

Now you might ask yourself, how does Fisk know so much when I talk to him? The answer is an easy one, Fisk has connections. More connections than I have. This city has eyes and ears everywhere and Fisk is connected to those eyes and ears constantly, which makes him a valuable asset to my work. Sometimes the information is not reliable but it gives me a start, which usually leads to something bigger. Then there were Russo's goons.

I had been so intent on finding Monica, Freddy *and* the notebook that I hadn't given much thought to Russo and his crew. In fact, I figured they were lying low, waiting for me to find the notebook so they could drop the hammer on me to get it back.

Fat lot of good it would do because once they tried there would be a lot of dead bodies drop and I would enjoy every minute of it. Russo and I have been at odds with each other ever since he took over for Sampson, the last boss here in the city. If the tale told is true, Russo killed his way up to Sampson's right hand man's job, Lenny, who died in a fiery crash while coming back from a delivery. The M.E.'s report called it an accident, a fuel line leaking and catching fire.

What the vine told was a different story. Seems that Lenny had words with Russo, and those words led to a beating. Lenny swore from his hospital bed that he would see Russo dead. Too bad for Lenny it didn't work out. As for Sampson, he was found shot in the head in his bed, a gun in his hand the only prints on it his.

Both Pat and I knew this wasn't right so we did some

checking until Pat was told to back off and I was told likewise by Pat whose ass was on the line if I dug any deeper. Oh, I still do a little digging from time to time, not enough to cause a stir, but one of these days I'm gonna find out who did him in and they will get theirs. I liked Sampson even if he was a hood.

He might have run the rackets here in town but he was a fair man, against any kind of hard drugs being sold by his people, maybe a little wacky weed but nothing in what he called the brain killing variety. No doubt his guys sold some on the sly but if they were caught they ended up either beat all to hell or sometimes in the hospital depending on the disciplinary action taken.

I headed back to the office to check on Shelly then made my way over to my old heap parked in the lot across from the office. I glanced in the back first before I opened the door; past experience telling me it was a good thing to do. I opened the door and crawled in, sat for a few moments then crawled back out, giving the car a once over before I crawled back in and started it up. I wouldn't put it past Striker to booby-trap my car in case the first one failed.

I drove down to Grant Street, turned left and made my way to Ralph's house, the address I got from Pat. Ralph's place is right across from the park, a white clapboard house with peeling paint and a sagging roof. I didn't expect him or Monica to be there, it had been at least three or four hours since the incident at the hotel and I'm sure they had boogied. Still, there might be a chance.

It was late afternoon as I pulled into the drive and cut my motor, the silence settling in around me made me uneasy. There was no car in the drive and none in the garage, so I crawled out of the car, unlimbered my .45 and eyed the house and its surroundings. Only the wind moaned through the eaves of the house and made a chill run up my back. I walked around to the corner of the house, paused as

I jacked a shell into the chamber just in case, the hammer cocked and ready as I moved toward the front porch.

At the steps I could see the front door was open a crack. Somewhere in the back of the house a light was on, probably in the kitchen, but nothing else, just dead quiet. I moved up the steps in a crouch, watched the windows on either side of the door. Any sign of movement and I would open up.

I got to the door; a smell touched my nose as I stood there, like over cooked meat burning. I slid over to the the door, eased open the screen then gave the door a nudge with the muzzle of my .45. The door opened without a sound. Nothing seemed to be moving in the room I looked into, dark shapes of furniture showed in the half-light, some big enough to hide a body who was waiting for the kill.

I eased in, the smell stronger. I took a step, my leg bumped into a small table, a lamp perched on it started to fall so I grabbed it. I took a deep breath, set it back in place and pulled the chain that turned it on. Only a small area was lit up by the lamp but it was enough as my eyes scanned the living room.

One hell of a fight had taken place in here; chairs overturned, small tables busted up, the couch knocked around and shoved into the wall but that was all, nothing slashed or piled in cone shapes. It was the fireplace where the smell was coming from, a body, its head laying in the dead coals of the fireplace. Whoever it was had been tied up, hands behind their back then the rest of the cord used to tie their feet together. The fire had been put out around the blackened head but some of the coals still had little wisps of steam coming off them. I checked the rest of the house out and found it empty.

I went back to the body and knelt beside it, knowing Ross would give me hell for moving it but I had to know so I raised it by one shoulder, the flesh on the shoulders crackling as I lifted it and the head dipped forward a little.

It was a man for one thing; no boobs showed on the chest and the face so seared and blackened it was unrecognizable. I let the body down slow, pretty much in the same place it had been and stood, looked around on the floor until I found the phone and told the operator to call the Station to see if Pat was around.

****

"Did you move the body?" Ross asked me as he knelt down beside what was left of the man. "And before you answer I know you did."

"Then why ask?" I grunted and lit my cigar, blowing smoke at him. Ross shook his head then rolled the body over, the face burned beyond recognition, the lips peeled back in a nasty smile. The eyes were gone, popped by the heat, a blackened strip of meat that once was a tongue was clamped between the teeth, almost bitten in two.

"He was shot also, looks like a small caliber to the back of the head, but whether it was before or after I couldn't tell you." Ross spoke in a soft tone poking at a small hole in the back of the head. "But I suspect after."

"Damn," Pat muttered and swallowed back the lump that had come up in his throat. "You think this is Ralph?"

"Unless he has dental records or prints on file somewhere I couldn't tell you. There's no ID on him." Ross stood, stripped the rubber gloves from his hands and told Wendell to get the rubber bag ready. Pat turned to me and motioned me to follow, the two of us walked a few feet away before he asked, "What about you, you think Freddy got him?"

"It's possible." I shrugged drawing more smoke. "It's possible, but if Freddy did get him where's Monica? I don't believe Freddy would have let her get away twice."

Pat nodded as I looked back over my shoulder at the body, my gut telling me that it wasn't Ralph. Pat nudged me with his elbow. I turned back toward him, my eyes narrowed.

"I know that look, what's up?"

"Just a feeling."

"Uh-huh and when you have those feelings bodies usually start to pile up," Pat grunted giving me his cop look.

I grinned, Pat mumbling under his breath something about having to put up with me. I knew deep in my gut that the body in the fireplace wasn't Ralph and I was damned sure it wasn't Freddy. Freddy wouldn't let an amateur get the best of him. Besides, Freddy was probably at a hood sawbones getting his face sewed back together. I asked Pat if he was done with me and he nodded, told me to get out of his sight as he turned and walked back to Ross and the others.

A lot of neighbors were braving the cold to see what the hell was going on so I took the long way around to my car to walk among them and listen. One guy, in a pea coat and wool trousers with a fat woman in a house dress and heavy coat, were jabbering to a uniform.

"Whoever they were," Pea Coat was saying, "they came barreling out of that house like the devil was after them. The guy had one hand wrapped up in a dishtowel, the damned rag was dripping blood and the woman was yelling at him to get in the car."

"What kind of car sir?" the uniform asked.

"39' Buick, the paint was black but faded in spots," Fatty said.

"And the woman, the woman had red hair," another woman cut in behind them. Fatty gave her a hard look but nodded.

"Did you get the tag number?" the uniform asked smiling slightly. He knew what was coming next.

"Well, I cain't see so well these days and ma here is about as blind as me so...," Pea Coat shrugged his shoulders. "But there was one thing, the car had a funny hood ornament on it, one of those kind you see on those fancy cars, a nude woman with wings all streamlined back like she was gettin' ready to take off."

I walked on to my car. A Buick with a Packard hood ornament on it shouldn't be too hard to find, especially in this town.

CHAPTER 11

That evening I told Fisk about the hood ornament and gave him the description of the car that had been given to the cop. He told me to give him a few days and he would get back to me. After that I went to get Shelly to take her out to a good dinner. I mean, Benny's is okay but I do believe she'd like to have something better than a ham sandwich, plus I wanted to see Jax to see if he knew anything.

I made a call to Jax Jazz over on McDaniel Street and asked Jax if he could squeeze us in for dinner. He told me to come on down, he would make a place. Jax Jazz used to be just a nightclub but a year ago he decided to put in a restaurant, the upstairs of the club having a large open room where he kept stuff stored.

Now it was a small restaurant, probably about ten tables in all, the décor staying with the Jazz theme. Rough brick walls with posters pasted to them, tables with linen tablecloths, a single candle in the center for mood and fancy chairs with padded bottoms to make your dining experience more pleasing. At least that's what Milt; Jax's bouncer told me one night while I was visiting Jax. Milt is the head honcho here on the upper floor but if things get rowdy, he's still the bouncer downstairs. He spends more time down in the club than upstairs, the service men being the cause of the rowdiness.

In his place, Rudy Wilson takes over as host. Rudy is a very sophisticated fellow with slicked back hair, a pencil mustache and a French accent to impress the diners, said accent as thin as his mustache. We left around seven and arrived around seven-thirty, getting through the door at a quarter of eight after I parked in the lot across from the club, arguing with the attendant over the price of parking. Seems it had risen from a dime during the day to twenty-five cents at night. I got him down to twenty cents and would have gotten it lower if Shelly hadn't paid him so she could eat.

"I'll swear," she poked me in the ribs as we crossed the street, "a girl could waste away by the time you dickered out a price."

"Well, we don't want that." I was hoping the remark didn't lead to her accusing me of saying she was fat. I'd been through that deal once before and didn't want to endure it again. Of course tonight, if anyone called her fat I would loosen some teeth.

Tonight she was dressed in one of those slinky gowns that hugged her body like a second skin, every hill and valley in bold relief, the deep V of her neckline drawing every normal male's eye the minute we got in range.

At the front door, my old buddy Jimmy grinned and shook my hand, pumped it was more like it, asked how I was and was about to ask about Shelly when he saw her. His mouth dropped open, then a silly grin crossed his face as he stepped back to let us in and winked at me, a soft spoken huba huba reached my ears. The next couple behind us tried to step on through behind us, Jimmy stopping them, frisked the guy and took his pop gun away from him. The guy complained about Jimmy not frisking me to which

Jimmy told him to either go on in or he could have his peashooter back and find another place to eat. The guy walked on in.

Yeah, I was packing but Jimmy knew me well enough to know it would stay in its home unless it was needed. Milt was at the foot of the stairs leading to the restaurant when he saw us coming, standing behind a walnut podium with one of those little lights hooked to it shining down on the reservation book. Milt is over six feet tall, broad shouldered and thick chested, his arms tight in the jacket he wore, a big smile plastered on his face which got even bigger when Shelly got closer. He ran his finger down the page then motioned us toward the steps with a wide wave of his hand bowing slightly as he did. I held back a chuckle, not wanting to ruin Shelly's evening by ending up out in the ally for pissing him off.

"Active night?" I asked him.

"So it would seem." He held out his arm slightly to Shelly to help her up the stairs. "Three servicemen causing trouble just found out that the alley is not a nice place."

He led us upstairs to our table and pulled out Shelly's chair when we reached it. She giggled and thanked him as she scooted in. Milt snapped his fingers and motioned for a waiter to make it quick. Our waiter was a short, skinny guy with a thin face and sharp nose, he had a pencil thin mustache on his upper lip, this one real, not fake and he tried, but failed to talk in a cultured voice, the Ozark's twang under it almost got a remark from me if Shelly hadn't kicked me under the table.

"May I recommend the Salmon." His voice made me grin again. Shelly gave me the eye over her menu as he added, "And maybe a salad before."

"No steak?" I gave him a questioning look.

"Well yes, we do have steak sir if that is what you prefer. How would you like it cooked?" I told him the fish would be fine and he took our menus, bowed slightly, then made tracks to turn the order in. Shelly kicked me under the table again then gave me the look and asked, "I wonder where Jax found him?"

"Probably in the soup line down at the kitchen." I grinned. "Or he's kin, probably the latter."

"So what is your next move?" She leaned over the table, her dress opening a little, her cleavage deepened.

"Are you talking about the case or when we leave here?" I eyed her; a lecherous smile crossed my lips.

"Oh, I know what will happen after we leave here." She gave me a seductive smile and wet her lips with the tip of her tongue. "I'm talking about the case."

"I've got Fisk checking out a few leads for me. Tomorrow I'm gonna go down and see Pat to see if they have an ID on who died at the house." I leaned back and was about to change the subject when the waiter appeared with a bottle of wine, showed it to us then pulled the cork. I told him I didn't order wine and he told me it was compliments of Jax, for the lady and me. I told him to thank Jax and he nodded as he poured.

"Do you think it was Ralph?" Shelly tasted the wine, her eyes looking at me over the edge of the wine glass.

"Maybe." I sampled the wine myself. It was white, a little dry but it was free so why complain. I mean, I could've had a beer and been just as happy.

"But you don't think it was?" Shelly leaned forward again, that seductive smile coming back.

"I'll know tomorrow." The salad came so we talked a little small talk then the fish came, a pretty good sized portion covered in some sauce that was okay but I could have done without it. I like fish, but just fish, nothing fancy poured or cooked on it. When we were done, we went down to the club, a Jazz band beginning to play, the room getting crowded with khakis and civvies. Jax caught me by the elbow as we looked for a table and led me back to his, helped Shelly get seated (at the same time getting a good look at her cleavage) then asked what we wanted.

Once he turned in our order, he sat down also, asked how the food was then leaned in close to me as Shelly sat drinking a gin and tonic listening to the music, me a Jack Daniels listening to Jax.

"Biscayne's man is out for blood Max." Jax spoke low close to my ear. "Farwell laid his scar open from his ear to the tip of his chin, about an inch longer than it was. I suppose you know Russo's men are tailing you."

"Yeah." I sipped the Jack as I nodded. "I ran into one of them in Kelso's so I sent a message back to Russo."

"So I heard." Jax nodded. "But did you know Biscayne has a few men watching you also, especially Shelly."

"Is that a fact?"

"Just watching her so far buddy but if you find the notebook first…" He let the words drop off.

I looked at Shelly and she looked back, smiled, kissed at me then went back to listening to the band, a slow fire started to burn in the pit of my stomach, one that would become a raging firestorm if anything happened to my kitten. Biscayne and Freddy both would be so full of lead it would take ten pallbearers on each coffin to carry them to their graves.

"In fact, one of her boys is sitting at the bar right now." Jax bobbed his head toward a skinny fellow with his fedora pulled down low over his eyes nursing a beer. He reminded me of a weasel waiting for the right moment to jump on his prey. I leaned in toward Jax and told him what I wanted to do. Jax nodded and stood, motioned for Milt who came over to the table, Jax whispering in his ear, Milt seating himself at the table with Shelly.

I stood as Jax slowly made his way toward the hood, his eyes watching. One of the waitresses after talking to Jax passed by the weasel, yelped and grabbed her butt.

"You son of a bitch!" she yelled then slapped him. The weasel reacted as I thought he would, coming off the stool cocking his fist, Jax suddenly behind him, the blue black barrel of a .45 shoved into his kidneys. Jax whispered in his ear and the weasel dropped his fist nodded and walked ahead of Jax toward his office, me following as Shelly give me a puzzled look. I patted the air for her to stay put.

I stepped into Jax's office, the weasel wanting to know what the hell was going on. He hadn't touched the girl. Then he saw me and his face paled.

"Mr. Black would like to have a word with you," Jax spoke, a nasty smile pasted on his face.

"It ain't gonna happen!" Weasel's hand dipped under his jacket as I stepped forward fast, my hand grabbed his wrist and jerked it from under the jacket, a .32 pistola coming out. I gave his wrist a squeeze and a twist as I grabbed the piece and jerked it from his hand.

"Looky here Jax." I flipped the pistol around in my hand and shoved the barrel into one of his nostrils. "Jimmy must have missed one."

"Yes he did." Jax opened the door and stepped half way out of it. "Why don't you enlighten our guest about the rule we have here, the one that applies to low life scum."

Jax chuckled as he stepped out the door and closed it, the weasel tried to jerk his head away so I pushed harder on the .32, a trickle of blood running down his upper lip.

"Freddy, where is he?" I growled at him.

"I don't know no Freddy." The Weasel's voice had a slight nasal whine to it, probably from the pistola jammed up his snout.

I gave the piece another shove. This time he whimpered, his upper lip smeared with blood and snot.

"One more time and if you tell me you don't know Freddy I'll pull the trigger, I don't think you want that do you?" I gave him my nastiest grin and he started to shake his head then stopped; any shaking might cause me to pull the trigger which would leave a mess on Jax's desk.

"So I ask again, where's Freddy?" I hissed at him, so

close I could smell the fear on his breath.

"I swear to God Black," he whined, his voice breaking, "I don't know where he hangs out; nobody does even Miss Biscayne."

"So what is he partial to?" I asked.

He gave me a funny look then his eyes lit up, he'd figured out what I meant.

"The guy is a freak, he likes pain, lots of pain, the more he can inflict the more he gets off on it. I heard the more they scream the better he likes it."

I had known men like that. Men who got sexual pleasure from being hurt or hurting someone so I had a good idea where Freddy boy might be hiding out. I took the muzzle out of Weasel's nose but still had his jacket gripped in my hand, the muzzle of the pistola lowered until it stopped at his crotch.

"Here's what I want you to do." I moved the gun close, touched the front of his pants where his balls would be, "I'm gonna let you go and you're gonna go back and tell The Bitch the same thing I told Russo. I see one of her flunkies tailing me I put a bullet in them. You, I put one somewhere else. Also, if anything happens to Shelly, I'll send The Bitch to hell where she belongs."

I gave the gun a push, the muzzle hit his bells and made his eyes bug, then I stepped away from him the piece still pointed below his waist, the Weasel holding himself as he backed toward the door.

"You bastard, I'll see you dead," he yelled at me.

"Yeah, I hear that a lot. Now leave before I change my mind." He yanked the door open, bolted out and ran into Milt and bounced off him. Milt grabbed his coat and pulled him toward the alley door, every time he tried to fight Milt, good old Milt popped him on top of the head, the dull thud of his fist almost loud enough to be heard above the music. I walked back to the table and slipped the .32 into my jacket pocket as I sat down across from Shelly who was on her third Gin and Tonic. I figured when we got home it was gonna be an all- nighter.

****

I woke about ten in the morning, a little hung over and still tired. As I said, it had been an all- nighter, Shelly drinking more Gin and tonics than I could count before I stopped her then tried to dance it out of her. It didn't work. I don't mind really. I mean, she is great in the sack but when she is drunk she gets wild. I sat up on the edge of the bed, rubbed my face with my hands and looked over my shoulder at her.

I stood, slapped her on the ass and bellowed out a good morning. I barely made it to the bathroom before things started flying through the air. Shelly gets mean when she has a hangover and from the amount of booze she had drank last night I suspect she had a doozy. I washed my face, combed my hair and thought about what the Weasel told me last night. Freddy was one of those sickos that got off on pain.

A doctor friend of mine once told me in laymen's terms that such people had an abnormal brain, a portion of it diseased at birth which caused them to have violent sexual tendencies. Still, there were others who weren't so violent, others who kept their fetish secret and hired others to help them play out their pain and domination fantasies. One of those who were in the business of doing this was Della Frost and from what I have heard about her nothing is too weird.

Della is a tall curvy woman with a waspish waist, slim hips, high, firm breasts she keeps pushed up so her cleavage shows when she wears her low necked dresses. She always dresses in black and some say she wears blood red under things beneath the black. She has a long face, not pointed, just long with a long nose and high cheek bones which some say give her a sensuous, but creepy look in the right light. Her lips are always painted a deep red, almost blood red and always looked wet and glistened. Her eyes are her trademark, dark brown, almost black, smoldering with secrets that made her a thing of beauty.

I have seen her only twice, once when Pat was questioning her about a murder and again on Commercial Street when she was in The Citizen's Drug, buying a few necessities. She had a seductive voice when she spoke, the kind that hinted at forbidden things she knew how to do. Shelly said she had seen her once, telling me she was nothing but a leather wearing whore and high priced to boot.

I opened the door just a crack and looked out at Shelly, the girl lay on her side facing the bathroom door, her eyes closed but I knew she was listening, waiting until I opened the door to attack. I grinned, opened the door a little more, her eyes opened to slits.

I slammed the door open and dove across the room just as a pillow came sailing toward my head. Her aim was too high and it passed over me, one end brushed my hair as I hit the bed, Shelly rolling out from under me before I slammed down on top of her. I was up before she could roll back and grab me, flipped her back on her belly and held her there as I straddled her. She arched her back and then straightened suddenly; her movement made me lose my grip on her as she twisted under me onto her back, her knee coming up stopping short of nailing my cajones.

"Good morning," she purred in a sweet voice. I laughed and rolled off of her.

"How's your head?" I asked her as she sat up and groaned.

"It's okay as long as I lay down." Another groan escaped her lips as she eased back on the bed. I chuckled, stood and dressed then told her to stay put; I was going down to make some coffee. She waved me off; another groan escaped her lips louder as the sudden movement brought her hangover into full play. I laughed as I headed to the door just as another pillow flew at me and bounce off the door as I closed it.

I turned on the hotplate in her office and got the coffee started, my mind going back to Della. Della migrated here from Chicago where she had quite a clientele. So why come here? Well, seems she was given a choice, either help the feds nail a certain crime boss who was one of her steady clients or go to jail for prostituting children. Seems one of her girls was only thirteen but the kid looked older, a lot older.

Well, Della had no use for jail so she agreed. So one crime boss bit the dust and Della, not her real name, came here. She was supposed to stay out of the business but that wasn't going to happen. She had expensive tastes and being a clerk in a five and dime just wasn't enough. I figure someday they will be onto her which will end her business along with her life.

Before that happens I need to make a visit to her house to see if she knows where Freddy is or if he has visited her little play house. My hope is he is staying there and this crap would be over. I was on my second cup of coffee when Shelly came down, well, shambled down the stairs, her eyes covered with sunglasses even though it was a cloudy day. I stood, poured her a cup of Joe, set it on the desk and plopped back down in her chair.

She sipped it, flinched then groaned. I took out the bottle of aspirin she had taken away from me earlier and set it in front of her; the girl snatched it up, shook six out in her hand, tossed them in her mouth then sipped her coffee again. I was about to make a comment when the door opened and Pat stepped in and stomped snow from his feet. Shelly jerked with each stomp.

"Well, good morning you two," his voice loud, accenting the words with a couple more stomps.

I nodded and Shelly just stared.

"I hear you two had a good old time last night?" He tipped his hat back as he sat down in one of the chairs in front of her desk.

"Well, one of us did." I snickered.

"How the hell…" she started to say then let the words cycle down.

"Oh, a little bird told me he pulled over a car last night, two people in it were very happy, especially the sexy lady giggling and running her hands through her man's hair." A big smile crossed Pat's face.

"Oh-my-God!" Shelly set the cup down on her desk then eased her butt down in the chair beside it.

"Oh yeah, he told me that he asked if there was anything he could do and this woman told him a police escort would be nice. She would like to get home in a hurry to tend to business." Pat fought back a laugh, clearing his throat to keep from it.

"Shit!" Shelly snapped under her breath, dropped her head and covered her face with her hands.

I stood and patted Shelly on the shoulder, her face turned up to me and even with the glasses I could tell her eyes were blazing. I looked at Pat and motioned for him to follow me into my office. Once we were inside, Shelly cut loose as the air turned blue in her office and I shut the door.

"You think she is a little upset?" Pat sat down in the chair by my desk and tipped his hat back and laughed.

"A little." I parked myself in my chair and chuckled. I remembered what happened last night, the cop, Sargent Perks could tell I was a lot more sober than she was but he still followed us home just in case.

"So what brings you here besides the ribbing of my favorite lady?"

"Well," he leaned forward a bit, "the body in the house wasn't Ralph. It was a cheap hood by the name of Lonny Ball. The way we figure it, he had broken into the house and either Ralph or Freddy came across him. If it was Freddy we can add another body to his count, if it was Ralph then the man's in big trouble."

"I'd say it was Ralph," I leaned back some, "trying to throw us off his scent. Making us think Freddy had gotten to him."

"Yeah, I figured the same." Pat nodded. "You find out anything else?"

"Well, I might have a lead on where Freddy is." I watched Pat as he leaned forward some more, his eyes narrowing, his voice lowering.

"And I suppose you're going to keep it to yourself?"

"No, but I need to do this one without any cop interference,"

"Where is he supposed to be?"

"Supposedly at Della Frost's place."

"The domination queen?"

I nodded then told him what had happened at Jax's club. He sat back in his chair, mulled it over in his mind for a few minutes then looked back up at me.

"Okay, and if he is there?"

"Then he is one dead mother."

"Now hold on buddy. The D.A. would like to have this guy alive. If you blow his brains out, which I suppose is your plan, then I have to answer for it plus it might be the last straw for you so to speak. Wellman has been looking for something to nail your ass on and this might just be it."

"I'll think about it."

"Damn it Max!"

"Trust me on this one Pat; I'll do everything in my power to give him a chance."

"Which with you is no chance at all."

I smiled and sipped my coffee again. Pat stood and glared at me as he leaned on my desk, both palms flat on top of it, his voice serious. "I agree with you Max. The bastard doesn't deserve a trial by jury but things are changing. The way you used to do things is not so in vogue these days. One of the assistant D.A.'s I know said Wellman is watching you, says at least once a day he hopes the hell he can end your type of justice so this city can feel safer."

I grunted and took another sip of coffee which was going on the cold side. My kind of justice Wellman called it. Most of the justice the courts hand out was sending men like Freddy to the nut hatch because some psychiatrist thinks he can make the man more useful in society; cure him of his urge to kill for the thrill of it.

I say bullshit to those types, the do-gooders who want to cure man's ills by exploring the mind, by taking the bad seed out of their brain and making *them* useful citizens. Men like Freddy are born like they are, no amount of scientific hoodoo is gonna change that. Their whole brain is a bad seed. The only thing they deserve is a bullet, end of story.

"You think Shelly is still upset?" Pat interrupted my thoughts as he went to the door. "It's awful quiet of there."

I shrugged as Pat opened the door a crack and peeked out to see if he could spot Shelly.

"Oh come on out you coward," she snapped at him.

"I'd hit the door fast if I were you."

"Yeah, right." Pat opened the door and gave her a quick wave as he made a fast exit from my office.

CHAPTER 12

Della's house was one of those Queen Ann style homes that were popular back in the 1890's. Located on West Palmer Street, the place is a rectangular, two story job with a gabled roof. The base of the house is Missouri granite with half round openings cut into the rock walls every so many feet. The front porch is well shaded and runs the entire front of the house. The length of porch on the east side of the house doesn't connect to the other section, a small door separating the two. Both porches have roofs over them with what they call Tuscan columns holding the roofs in place.

The steps at one time were of the same granite as the foundation and looked as if they were polished but the years and the elements had worn the shine off of them so what remains is just a gritty, hard surface.

I mounted the steps and walked up to the door, a recessed job with beveled glass sidelights with windows on either side. I could tell the door had been replaced, the one hanging on the hinges jet black, a silver knocker in the shape of a whip decorating it. I gave it a knock and waited.

After a minute I knocked again, this time with my fist, the knocker jumped with each pound on the door. I was about to do it again when it swung open, a short, redhead stood there in a fleece bathrobe blinking the sleep out of her eyes.

She probably was a little over five feet, a little on the chubby side with cherubic cheeks and hair red as fire. It was a dye job because her roots were beginning to peek out and blue-green eyes drilled holes in me.

"Business hours are from seven p.m. until whenever, come back then." She started to close the door so I slammed my arm against it and gave it a shove, her short legs churned backwards as her hand came out from under her robe with a small automatic. I grabbed her wrist and gave it a twist; her mouth opened in a yelp, the gun falling to the floor. That was when her foot came out from under the robe aimed at my crotch.

I jerked my leg in front of it; my thigh blocked her foot, numbed it for a second as I stepped in and slapped her hard across the face. This time she took a swing and I blocked it, so I slapped her again, her head jerking so hard to the left I thought her neck would break. She hissed like a snake, her eyes locked on mine flashing fire. She tensed and I drew back again, this time I made a fist, a voice from behind her froze us both.

"You're wasting your time Mr. Black. Nora likes being beaten, it gets her off."

Nora smiled a wicked smile as I let go and she stepped back and wiped the blood off her lips. Della stepped around her, wrapped in a silk robe as black as night, her platinum blond hair and pale skin made her look like a ghost in the dim entryway. She smiled as she walked past me, closed the door then walked back in front of me and dismissed Nora with a wave of her hand.

"Now Mr. Black, let's get out of this cold entryway to where it's warmer." Della turned and walked down a short hall to a sitting room on the left. From what I could see the house still retained the charm of the last owner's wife, a warehouse owner who had been into imports and bootlegging, the bootlegging keeping his wife in money to decorate the house until a rival gang took him out one night as he and his men unloaded a shipment.

The room was well lit with three windows, the walls paneled with dark wood and trim. The floor that parquet stuff. A big fireplace burned brightly as the social elite would say, warming the room so well I pulled my trench coat off and tossed in on a chair. The room was decorated nicely, the chairs over stuffed with dark blue velvet covers and one of those couches with the back shaped in an S, you know the kind where the lady sits on one side and the man on the other so they can keep their hands to themselves.

Two chairs sat in front of the fireplace and Della floated into one then motioned for me to take the other. As I sat down she smiled at me, her face framed by hair that fell to her shoulders, her lips slightly parted, her eyes checking me out. It gave me the creeps.

"Now Max," her voice held a seductive tone, "what are you here for?"

"Fredrick Striker."

"I see, and what makes you think he is here?"

"He likes pain, both on the giving and receiving, which you deal in."

"I see. So you think that since I deal in such, he might be residing here?"

Della leaned toward me, her eyes narrowed for a second as her hair fell over her face a little, casting a shadow over it which made her look devious. I leaned forward also; my eyes drilled into hers as my voice took on a low and nasty tone.

"Look Della, unless you want Pat and his boys coming in here tearing this place apart, you better come clean with me."

Another pause, this one filled the air with tension.

Della's eyes narrowed, a deadly look filling them.

"Striker did come here." She spoke in the same seductive tone only softer, deadlier. "Nora paired up with him but he wanted to use his own toys. So when I asked him if I could see them first, he refused and got angry, claimed he would pay more than the standard fee. I told him it made no difference what he paid, I needed to see what he used and he cursed, told me I knew nothing about domination and left."

I leaned back and shook my head. Freddy was one sick puppy and Della realized it and didn't want any of her girls either hurt or dead, refusing to let him in unless he showed her his own personal equipment which I knew was of his own devising.

"Okay, but if I find out you've lied to me..." I brought my voice back to normal as I stood. Della stood also, like a cat uncoiling from a long nap, her eyes still a little narrowed but there was a smile on her face, a cold smile that made me want to dip my hand under my jacket just in case.

"Let me assure you Mr. Black, we are very refined at what we do here. Such trash as Striker is not welcome in this house." I turned and picked up my trench coat and slipped it on, her figure never left the corner of my eye.

"Nora will see you out." She motioned toward the hall. The redhead was standing in the doorway, her eyes still narrowed and that cold smile got even colder.

"Thank you for your time," I grunted as I walked toward Nora, the redhead stepped out of the way for me to pass. I stopped in the doorway and motioned for her to go ahead. Nora smirked then walked ahead of me, my hand now going under my jacket, touching the butt of my .45. At the door Nora opened it; a cold draft whipped in and made her pull the robe tighter around herself. I nodded at her and when I was even with her she leaned in slightly, her voice a whisper.

"One of the girls who works here, Vicky Taylor, she was in the room when Striker was here. She hasn't showed up in a couple of nights. We were close." She still had that cold smile on her face but her eyes had softened a little.

I nodded then stepped out the door, the heavy panel closing behind me, the wind picked up as I walked back to my car. Della said they were refined in what they did. If inflicting pain was refined I must be doing one hell of a job because I inflicted a lot of it when I worked a case, just not in the way she does it.

*****

I called Pat and asked if he was gonna be in his office. He told me he was so I told him to stay put, I'd be right there. I drove to the Police Department building on Market Street or what is more commonly known as "The Station". I always wondered about that and asked a couple of old timers where it came from. One of them told me it was called that back in the twenties because at that time they had only one cell in the building, a criminal coming in and charged, then taken to the Greene County Lockup hence The Station moniker being given because their stay was short.

In the mid-thirties it had been added on to, extensions off the right side of the building with a basement, more cells and a couple of interrogation rooms. This building had a second floor, the second story held Pat's office and a squad room for his detectives. I took the staircase up to the second floor and stepped into the squad room, what detectives Pat had left at their desks filling out paper work.

Stiller, one of his older detectives was at his desk pounding on an ancient typewriter, cussing it under his breath when the keys stuck. He looked up when I passed and shook his head. The guy looked seventy but was in his mid-fifties, his face heavily lined, his knuckles scarred from past years of breaking up fights in bars.

"How's it going Stiller?" I paused by his desk and offered him a cigar.

"Nothing to my liking," he growled back and smiled as he clipped the cigar between his fingers. "I hate paperwork. How about you, any leads on that Striker fellow?"

"Bits and pieces." I struck a match and lit him up.

"Hu-huh," Stiller grinned blowing smoke, "You wouldn't josh an old detective would you?"

"Never." I held up my hands and took a step back. He chuckled and went back to pounding, the keys jamming together, a stream of cuss words coming out as he hit the typewriter with the heel of his hand, the keys fell back, Stiller continuing.

Pat was on the phone when I walked in. He motioned for me to sit down as he listened on the phone. There were a few uh-huhs and a yes sir, the look on his face sour as if he had bitten into a lemon. I took out a cigar, clamped it in my teeth, took a match from my pocket and lit up as he hung up the receiver.

"Well, that was our friend Wellman," the lemon look still on his face. "He says the newspapers are harassing him every other hour about the Stedman murders telling him the people have a right to know if a maniac is on the loose. They also want to know who it was that was found in the Stedman house with his face burned off. He said he needs answers and he needs them now."

I settled back in my chair and blew smoke in the air. Pat eyed me waiting.

"I went to see Della." I inspected the end of my cigar as I spoke, "No Striker but he had been there."

"And?" Pat leaned forward; a frown grew on his face.

"She turned him out." I clamped the cigar back between my teeth. "He didn't want to use her toys, had brought his own and when he wouldn't let her look them over she told him no."

"A lot of help that is," Pat growled.

"Uh-huh, but a chubby redhead told me on the sly before I left that he was eyeing one of the girls, a Vicky Taylor. She said she hadn't been in for a couple of nights. Got anything on her?"

Pat picked up the phone and dialed down stairs, talked to Gabby for a moment then hung up.

"It'll be a few minutes." Pat crossed his hands over his belly.

"Gabby still mad at you?" I took the cigar out of my mouth and rolled it between my fingers.

"Kinda," his voice was low as he spoke. "She didn't speak to me for a couple of days but I managed to scare up a Hersey bar and that seemed to thaw her out a little."

"You outta ask her out." I looked at him. "Take her to dinner, to a movie, who knows what might happen, you might get lucky?

"Yeah, well, I might if I…" He froze in midsentence, his face going red and his eyes shifted to the doorway.

"Might what?" Gabby stood in the doorway, her hands on her hips.

"Well, uh…" Pat's face was getting redder.

I grinned and turned my head toward her. Gabby walked in and lay a file on his desk. She nodded at me then turned back to Pat.

"I swear, some men are just so thick headed." She stared at him, hands going back on her hips. "Do you want to go out or not?"

Pat's face went beet red and I had to bite my lip to keep from laughing out loud. She had heard the conversation.

"Well, yes, yes I do," he stuttered.

"Good." She smiled at him. "This Friday, come over to the house, I'll feed you then we can pick a movie out of the paper."

"Yeah." He had a goofy grin pasted on his face which

made me snort trying to stifle a laugh.

"Don't be late." She shook a finger at him then spun on her heels and walked out humming a tune to herself. After she exited the squad room I burst out laughing, even old Stiller joined in.

"Looks like you got a date, and don't be late!" I shook a finger at him

Pat gave me the evil eye as he picked up the file and opened it.

"Vicky Taylor." He cleared his throat and glanced out at Stiller who was still laughing. "Picked up on prostitution numerous times before she went to Della's, arrested once for drug possession and paid a fine, disturbing the peace twice, this being when she was living with her boyfriend, that's about it, nothing serious."

"There an address?"

"Yeah, she lives over on Grant across from the school or did, that's her last address," Pat said as he closed the file.

"You up for a road trip?"

"You asking me to go with you?"

"You want to go or not?" I stood and rolled the cigar from one side of my mouth to the other and gave him an impatient look.

"Hell yes!" He grabbed his coat, Stiller still snickering as we passed by his desk.

CHAPTER 13

Vicky Taylor's house was a rent job, the reason you could tell this was because it was kept up just enough to keep the neighbors happy and off the landlord's ass. Most of the paint was chipped away in places and the front walk of field stone was missing a few stones. The windows were bare, no screens or plastic and the curtains were drawn. The front porch was small, a little rickety, the two steps leading to the porch split and weathered. The porch itself was grayed from the weather. In one spot the wood had rotted and was splintering up.

The front door looked fairly sturdy having been painted so many times the paint had peeled away and spots of past colors shown through. I tested the floor in front of the door, the wood here worn and flaking away but it seemed to be solid so I stepped up and knocked, then knocked again, this time harder. Pat nodded for me to try again and went off the porch and peeked into the windows trying to see in the house between the cracks in the curtains.

I knocked again, this time calling out Vicky's name.

When nothing happened I gripped the doorknob and gave it a turn. I opened the door just a crack, the soft sound of footsteps coming from the other side. I grabbed my .45 and looked at Pat who had come back on the porch, his .38 gripped in his hand. He nodded as I pushed the door open and ducked low which was a good thing I did, two shots split the air, hissed over the top of my fedora and barely missed Pat.

I ducked beside the couch, aimed at where the last shot came from and pulled off three, moving the muzzle of my .45 in a short arch, one hit some glass in the kitchen, the other knocked out the backdoor glass, the other ripped a cabinet door almost off its hinges. I bolted forward, coming up next to the wall of the doorway next to the kitchen with just enough wall to give me some cover, Pat making it to the other side with about the same amount. Someone moved in the kitchen, the sound of glass crunched under their feet loud.

"Striker, give it up!" I yelled.

Four more shots tore hunks out of the door jamb then the back door slammed open, the screen door torn off its hinges as a body exited the kitchen. I stepped out and pulled the trigger, my two shots hissed through empty air. Pat was headed toward the front door as I ran through the kitchen, and out the back door, my .45 ready just in case. The yard was a small one, a board fence running from one side of the house to the other, a gate in the back of it swinging in the wind as I crossed the yard and looked out in the alley running behind the house. I jerked my head back just in time, the blast of a pistol and the slam of a slug tore some of the wood from the fence and splattered my face with splinters.

I looked back at the house to see if Pat had come back through but he wasn't there. Suddenly, I heard Pat yell, two shots fired from the other side of the fence then silence. I ran in the direction of the shots, rounded the fence to see

Pat leaning against it, his face twisted his gun hand limp by his side. I made a fast run at him just as he slid down to the ground, his voice low, muttering curses.

"Hey buddy." I knelt beside him. He looked up at me and groaned. A shiv, thin bladed, the handle round and black stuck from his shoulder.

"The little bastard is fast." His hand touched the knife handle and he flinched. "I was coming down beside the fence when he rounded the corner. He raised his hand and I fired twice, the knife he threw hit my shoulder the second after I fired my second shot. He took off across the yard there and was gone." Pat nodded toward the yard behind me.

"Did you hit him?" I asked as I looked the knife wound over.

"I don't know." Pat flinched as I touched the blade and moaned, "Jesus that hurts!"

"Sorry." I helped him sit up a little more, pain twisted his face. "I'll call for an ambulance and..."

We both heard the sirens before I could finish my sentence so I asked him if he was good for a minute. He nodded and told me to see if Striker left a blood trail. I nodded and walked across the open yard just as a cop car skidded to a halt in the alley, two uniforms jumped out and headed toward Pat.

****

The blade was eight inches long and sharp as a razor. It had entered the muscle between Pat's collar bone and chest, nicking the bone. The doc who took it out said he was lucky because he thinks the blade was intended for Pat's neck. I nodded and knew it was but one of Pat's bullets had thrown off Striker's aim. I found a blood trail leading across the open yard to the street, and then it disappeared.

The boys found Vicky in the house, tied to the bed. At

first they thought she was dead, the sheets bloody and numerous cuts all over her body. One of them felt for a pulse and Vicky's eyes snapped open. She tried to scream around the ball gag in her mouth, a homemade job made from a child's rubber ball and a piece of black cloth punched through the center.

When they got it off of her and her arms and legs untied she let out a wail, grabbed one of the ambulance attendants crying, thanking him for getting her away from the devil. Most of the cuts were not deep, just deep enough to cause a lot of pain; her screams drowned out by the ball gag in her mouth. The only bad wound she had received was a patch of skin taken off her breast, a strip about three inches long including the nipple. She was in surgery now getting that bit of flesh taken care of.

Pat was down in emergency still, the doc giving him a couple of stitches and a tetanus shot, just in case. I was in the waiting area, the same nurse I had a run in with on another case tending the desk, watching me, telling me if I even attempted to go back there she would put my lights out. I do believe she could too.

After about an hour plus one cup of god awful coffee, Pat came out in a wheelchair, growling the whole time he could walk thank you very much.

"He gonna be okay?" I asked the nurse who pushed him.

"His shoulder yes, his dignity, no." She rolled her eyes and left him with me and gave me that you deal with him look.

"Did I get that son of a bitch?" he growled at me.

"Yeah, but he got away."

"Well, he was damned lucky, I had a bead on him right between the eyes when he threw the knife and spoiled my aim. Damn, this is gonna hurt like hell once the drugs wear off."

"Yeah, believe me I know." I grabbed him as he stood

and tried to take a step and stumbled a bit.

"You're supposed to be in the damned chair until I release you," a voice growled behind us. I looked over my shoulder and a doctor was headed our way, a pill bottle in his hand, a scowl on his face.

"Look." Pat turned toward the doctor. "I've got shit to do and…"

"And you'll go home tonight, get some sleep and take one of these every four hours for pain," he growled as he shoved the pills in Pat's coat pocket.

"But the girl," Pat started to say.

"I'll check on her." I motioned to one of the uniforms standing by the door. "You do what the doc says."

"Yeah, like you would do that." He glared at me.

"Take him home," I told the uniform. "Tie him to the bed if you have to but make sure he stays there. I know, call Gabby and tell her, her date is gonna be canceled Friday and why, I'm sure she will see he is up to snuff to keep it."

"Oh, thanks a lot." He tried to sound disgusted as a smile crept up on the corners of his mouth telling me different.

"You keep me informed." Pat pointed his good arm at me as the uniform led him out the door.

"Count on it." I turned back to the doc and asked, "Vicky, she out of surgery yet?"

"We can find out, but I doubt she will be awake enough to answer questions." He walked up to the nurse's desk and leaned on it, the nurse behind it turned toward him. "Linda, call up to surgery and see if Vicky Taylor is out of the cutting room yet."

The red headed nurse turned around, her eyes locked on mine, a grunt coming from her throat.

"You two have met I assume?" The doc chuckled.

"Yeah we have." I made a kissing sound at her as she picked up the phone and dialed an extension.

****

Vicky looked like one big cut from head to toe. Most of them were superficial wounds, shallow but painful. A few were deeper, these were the ones given a few stitches. The biggie was her breast. The doc said the skin had been flayed off the top, across and down the underneath side of the breast, the nipple cut completely off.

I flinched when he told me that. It was be like being told a fellow's bells had been relieved from his body. He said she was still under sedation and probably would be out the rest of the night. I thanked him and found a phone, called Shelly to tell her where I was gonna be for the next few hours then told her to bolt the doors, lock the windows and keep her .38 cocked and ready.

Then she asked if she could come down and be with me. I thought it over for a second then decided it might be a good idea so I said yeah and told her I would send one of Pat's patrolmen to pick her up. A couple of uniforms stood at the nurse's station talking, one of them I knew, a fellow by the name of Preston, a straight up guy who had worked the Commercial Street beat a while before he got transferred to the Square.

I asked him if he would mind going to get Shelly, that I would be more comfortable if she was with me. He told me yeah and took off. The other cop, a lean faced man with a pointed nose and chin nodded at me then turned back to the nurse behind the desk, the nurse looked at me and rolled her eyes. I chuckled under my breath and walked to the waiting room across from the desk and stepped inside.

There were a couple of civilians in the room, one a middle aged lady in a worn gray wool dress with a matching gray hat, a hanky wiping at her eyes every so often. The other was a tall, lanky guy, over six feet with slicked back hair, khakis, a blue work shirt and a leather jacket on. His hat was a little beat up and was pulled over his eyes, his chest rising and falling slowly in sleep.

The last two in the room were cops, a couple of Pat's detectives, Morris Paton and his buddy Jim McCall. They had been talking when I opened the door but stopped and gave me the eye as I walked over to the coffee urn and drew a cup. Paton was a short skinny fellow, his suits not quite fitting him well, the overcoat covering the suit a little too long in the sleeves. McCall was a fat man about an inch shorter than Paton. The guy had to weigh at least 290, 295, his suit was a little tight, not much but enough to make the vest he wore strain at the buttons.

Both had the tell tale bulge under their coats, Paton's under his arm, McCall's at his belt. I sipped the coffee and made a face. Hospital coffee always tastes like it is two days old or at least it does to me so I poured some sugar in it and at the same time watched the two detectives out of the corner of my eye.

Rumor was that the two of them had connections to Russo. Inside information such as the raids that Pat sometimes set up on Russo's gambling dens being passed by them to Russo's men at a price. Of course nothing could be proved but still, the insinuation was there. As I stirred the sugar in my diesel fuel the two of them conversed in low tones and every once in a while glanced my way. I let a small smile touch my lips as I turned and walked over to one of the vinyl chairs and plopped down in it, set my coffee cup on the table next to me and picked up the evening newspaper.

I had just started to read the column my sometimes buddy Andy Henderson wrote about the escalating crime in the city, his reference to vigilante justice being aimed my way. I was halfway through it when I saw Paton break away from his buddy and saunter over to where I sat, eased himself into a chair beside me and cleared his throat.

"Something on your mind Paton?" I asked never

looking away from the paper.

"Yeah." He leaned in close, his breath smelled of bad teeth and cigarette smoke. "Rumor has it that there is a notebook involved in all of this. Is that true?"

I shrugged and kept reading the paper.

"You know if there is and you're withholding information we could run you to the Station and keep you for a while." A smile crossed his face as he leaned in closer.

"You could, but it wouldn't do you any good." I turned to look at him, a nasty smile on my lips. "Besides your buddy already knows I'm after the book so why threaten me with the rubber hose treatment."

Paton's face went red at the mention of this and my smile widened as I looked at him, our eyes locked, his smile disappearing.

"Besides, your boss thinks I already have it," I added.

"Well do…" Paton started to say then stopped. You could almost see the steam coming from his ears as I chuckled and went back to reading my paper. Paton stood; his hands clenched in fists, his breathing heavy.

"Let's go shamus," he hissed at me.

I folded the paper closed and stood. Paton reached in his pocket for a pair of cuffs just as the door opened and Pat walked in, Shelly close behind him.

"What the hell are you doing Paton?" Pat bellowed at him, the two civvies in the room jumped, the guy asleep almost fell out of his chair.

"I'm…" Paton started to say just as McCall stepped up beside him, laid a hand on his partner's shoulder and gave it a squeeze.

"Just a little misunderstanding Cap." McCall smiled as he patted.

"Uh-huh, don't you two have somewhere to be?" Pat growled at them.

"Yes, yes we do." McCall grabbed Paton's arm before

he could say anything and pulled him toward the door. Paton tried to jerk away from him and McCall tightened his grip.

"Then be there!" Pat hissed at the two of them. Paton muttered something as McCall pushed him out the door, Pat turning to me, his arm in a sling, his face showed some pain.

"I thought you were supposed to go home." I grinned. "But I'm glad you came back."

"Yeah, well when I heard those two were supposed to stay the night here I decided to come back." Pat eased down in the chair Paton was parked in. The corners of his mouth tightened as he repositioned the arm then he let out a sigh.

"I got a man on her door, which those two didn't have and those pills the damned doctor gave me only dull the pain," his voice tight as he spoke.

I pulled up another chair for Shelly then settled into mine and asked, "Did you look in on her?"

"Yeah." Pat made a face. "Striker is psychotic. A guy has to be a monster to do that to a woman?"

I wondered the same thing myself. Striker *was* a monster, a monster with a rotten brain. If I have my way though, that brain was gonna pop like a rotten melon once I get done with him.

"What were those two up to?" Pat shifted in his chair toward me, another twist of pain showed on his face.

"Nothing but bullshit as usual."

"Bullshit or not, Paton was gonna take you in, why?"

"He said I was withholding information about the notebook."

"Like I don't already know that?"

I held up my hands in that "what, me?" gesture and Shelly snickered. Pat glared at me, his mouth a thin line on his face only broken when pain crossed it.

I nodded. "Yes, it was about the notebook, they were

gonna sweat it out of me at the Station, or take me to someone who would, probably the latter."

"Yeah, I wish I could prove that."

"You just might before this is over."

Pat nodded then wished he hadn't, a flash of pain twisting his mouth. I told him to relax, that I'd check on the guard at the girl's door and stood. Shelly was reading a magazine, one of those movie magazines that wrote the latest crap about the stars. Pat was nodding off, the pain pills, which I knew would kick in sometime or the other were taking effect.

I took off my trench coat and covered him with it, he mumbled something then his chin settled on his chest. Pat and I have known each other only a short time but the guy was a straight up Irish Joe, by the book most of the time but not going by it all the time. He is a tall man, with thick red hair and a red mustache. He wears off the rack suits that seem to fit him pretty good and his fedora is the most expensive of his clothing.

He carries a snub nosed .38 under his arm and is fast. I accused him of practicing in front of the mirror once and got a dirty look for it. The guy works all the time, his job being one to keep him at the Station sometimes twenty-four hours a day with the war having shorted him on manpower. Many is the time I have told him he needs to lighten up, find himself a nice girl or maybe a not so nice one to take some of the tension off of him. This usually leads to an argument and Pat gets mad, tells me to mind my own business; he is waiting for the right girl.

I usually answer him with okay then tell him until the right one comes along he needs to play the field and sample some of the not so right ones. This only makes him madder and closes the conversation. I asked Shelly if she was packin'. She nodded then I told her to be alert, walked to the door and opened it, the hallway quiet, a knife thudding into the wall inches from my head as I stepped out.

****

Striker was dressed like a patient but one of his pant legs had dipped a little below the hem of his hospital gown which gave him away. I took off in a run, glanced at the nurse's desk and saw that she was slumped over on it, out but not dead, no blood seeped onto the papers under her. Striker rounded the corner as I sprinted down the hall, my .45 out and cocked. As I rounded the corner, another orderly stepped from a room with a tray in his hands. Striker slammed into him the tray flying. It was a dinner tray, plates and food everywhere.

I was about to pull off a shot when another door opened and a nurse stepped out. I yelled and she froze, I cursed and shoved her out of the way, trying to avoid the food on the floor and missed. The potatoes and gravy did me in, my foot connected with the slick crap sending me sprawling to the floor, Striker looking back, his laugh echoing in the quiet hallway.

As I sat up, Shelly ran around the corner, her .38 out as she came toward me.

"Are you hurt?" she asked helping me up.

"Only my pride kitten." I shook some crushed peas off my hand.

The orderly groaned and stood up and rubbed his head where he had thumped it against the wall. A couple of doctors were coming down the hallway; one checked the nurse and the other me. I told him I was alright and he went to the orderly. Shelly peeled my jacket off and took it to a bathroom to see if she could clean it off.

I followed her and waited until she came out, Striker might still be around and I didn't want him doubling back to get hold of Shelly. As I waited with the door open, Pat walked up, and asked if I was alright.

"No." I grunted at him. "What about Vicky, is she

alright?"

"Yeah, I suspect you stepped out just as he was about to slit the nurse's throat." I nodded in agreement just as Shelly came out of the bathroom and handed me my jacket.

"You're gonna have to send it to Sawyer." I inspected the wet spots on it and nodded, Sawyer being my dry cleaner.

"I'm doubling the guard with what people I can," Pat said as he followed me down the hall, "I wish you could have put one in him like I did. Yours would have knocked his ass down."

"Well, I would have if it hadn't of been for the nurse stepping out of the room." I shook my head as I slid my jacket back on. "Either way I have a slug with his name on it."

Pat went back to check on the nurse and the uniform by Vicky's door again. As he left, he told me and Shelly to go home and get some sleep. If anything happened he would call. I told him he should do the same but he shook his head and tried to shoo us out. I shook my head and told him to forget it, he needed me and Shelly to stick around. He started to say something again and I cut him off, told Shelly to go question the nurse and started my round of the hospital to find out how that son of a bitch got in.

CHAPTER 14

I woke up in a cold sweat; the images still rampaged through my mind from my nightmare. I was running down a long hallway, the walls and floors white, the hallway seemed to go on forever, stretched out in front of me like a never ending tunnel. At the end of that tunnel, I could see Striker, laughing and grinning, throwing knives at me as I bobbed and weaved to avoid them. But that wasn't the nightmare part, the nightmare part was as one hand was tossing knives at me, the other was skinning Shelly, stripping off body length strips of flesh and hung them on a clothesline, Shelly screaming, begging him to stop.

I sat up on the edge of the bed and rubbed my face hard, the images faded but the fear of this actually happening hung on. I mean, I know the cops were stretched out but the ones Pat had placed on duty were some of the best so how did Striker get past them? They had been briefed, his picture shown to them and they had been told he had been cut in a fight; still he had used a good disguise, a hospital patient which made sense. I mean, who would question a fellow who wandered around in a hospital gown with a bandage covering his jaw?

I got up, Shelly moaned a little but stayed asleep. We had spent most of the evening and night at the hospital. She questioned the nurses while I checked on possible holes this bastard could have crawled through. All Pat and I could figure was there was an insider, someone who worked there that was on Biscayne's payroll but to find that out meant more questions, more hours of no sleep. I had my suspicions who had cleared the way for Striker to get in. Biscayne's money was just as spendable as Russo's.

I figured since Striker had botched this attempt to kill Vicky, if that was who he was after, he would probably wait until things died down before he tried again, probably when Vicky was released and sent home. Then he would do it all over again, only this time we might not be able to catch him. He would be on guard and a bastard like Striker who is on guard is a very dangerous fellow.

Then of course there was Shelly.

I know she is capable of handling herself with most crooks but this guy is beyond crook. I only knew of one other man who liked his work so well, Myer Belasco, a tall, spooky man who reminded you of one of those undertakers you saw in the movies. If he had went to Hollywood he would have been a shoe in. With Myer though it was strangulation after he had burned the victim numerous times with hot irons and anything else that caught his fancy,

His last victim was the one who had done him in. She had slipped out of the ropes he had her tied up with, waited until she heard him coming back then used his own blowtorch to set him on fire just before she drove a hot iron through his right eye and into his brain.

But Striker is a different breed. He is like a shadow, coming and going, leaving bodies in his wake. I don't want Shelly to be one of those bodies. I walked to the big easy chair by the radio and sat down, wondering how I could get her out of harm's way without her pitching a fit which wasn't going to be easy.

But if that bastard got hold of her...

I got up and walked over to the table, a bottle of whiskey sat there along with a couple of glasses. I poured and downed it, got ready to pour another when I heard something thump on the stairway. Shelly heard it too because I saw her head jerk on the bed then she rolled over, looked at me as I held a finger up to my lips. I stepped over and relieved my .45 from its home, half jacked the slide back to see if there was one in the chamber, then let it down slowly and cocked the hammer. Shelly was on the edge of the bed getting up, the nightgown she had on was a little thin and showed a lot of what she had as she crossed behind me and opened what looked like a jewelry box, inside it was the .32 auto I had liberated from Biscayne's boy.

She checked it and cocked the hammer as I went to the door. One good thing about the door, it opened out onto the landing instead of into the room. The minute the knob was turned I could hit it and knock whoever was on the other side on their ass. I waited nothing but silence for a few minutes then another thump, the knob jiggled a little then turned.

When the latch clicked free of the jamb I hit the door hard, a short yelp came from the other side as a body slammed into the wall across from it. I stepped out fast, my .45 ready to blast brains when a woman's voice yelled and told me not to shoot. A short body lay crumpled against the wall, breathing heavy and moaning. I hit the light switch at the top of the stairs and the stairway lit up, a chunky redhead staring up at me, her eyes filled with fear, her face a swollen mask of flesh.

Shelly pushed past me and knelt beside the woman before I could tell her to stop. I saw the glitter of the knife and so did she, the blade arched up, Shelly jerked back, the blade point skimming the side of her cheek but her quick motion sent her back too far, her body tumbled ass over tea kettle down the steps.

That was when I saw the shadow through the glass in the door, the door being pushed open. I growled an oath and brought the muzzle of my .45 up, firing at the shadow, the door glass shattered, some of the slugs slammed the wood around the door and the shadow took a powder.

I was down the steps in three seconds, ducked out the door in a crouch and scanned the sidewalk then stepped back in to check Shelly over, her body lying in a twisted heap but she looked okay. I patted her cheek a couple of times and she groaned, her eyes fluttered open, and she smiled at me.

"Do you hurt anywhere kitten?" I asked her. She shifted then took in a sharp breath.

"My leg," she gasped. I nodded and looked them both over, one looked okay but the other had an ugly bulge at the thigh.

"Just lay still." I stood mounting the steps. "I'll call an ambulance. Shoot anything that shows itself in the doorway." I had found her the .32 halfway down the steps and handed it to her. Shelly nodded and watched the door.

I went back upstairs to make the call since I didn't have my keys on me to unlock the office and also to check on Nora who was still laying against the wall. She was still out so I made the call, told the operator to send an ambulance to my address then hung up then contacted the Station to tell Pat Peterson, if he was in, there had been an accident here then hung up. I walked over to where Nora lay and knelt beside her, her eyes slits watching me. I grinned a wicked grin and shoved the .45 under her chin, her eyes popped open then narrowed, the knife in her hand coming up, slicing my undershirt as I jerked back, the blade just missing my throat. I grabbed it with my free hand, my smile getting wicked nasty as I raised the .45 and rapped her on the head with the muzzle. She grunted and her eyes rolled up into her head as she passed out.

I went back down to make Shelly as comfortable as possible then checked the sidewalk again making sure no one was skulking around. My kitten was showing a lot of pain on her face and some tears in her eyes. I waited until the ambulance came and they had her loaded on it before I spoke.

"I need to see what I can get out of the bitch on the landing, okay?" I caressed her cheek, caught one of the tears on my finger tip and kissed it.

"Y-yes." She blinked out more tears. "Go make the bitch talk."

I told her I would be with her as quick as I could, leaned down and kissed her forehead before I walked back up the stairs to where Nora was. I stepped in front of her, reached down and grabbed the front of her coat and jerked her to her feet. Nora's eyes opened wide, her lips trembling.

"Please," she whispered from swollen lips, "I had to."

"Uh-huh." I pulled her over to the table we sat at for supper, jerked out a chair and slammed her fat ass into it then told her if she moved, her lips would be a hell of a lot fatter than they already were. Tears streamed from her eyes and she breathed in short gasps. I started to pull her coat open but she grabbed it, her eyes pleading with me to not look. Then I saw the drops of blood dripping on the floor from under the coat. I dragged out the other chair, turned it backwards and leaned on the back, my .45 still gripped in my hand.

"What did he do to you?" I asked. Her lips trembled more as she let out a sob, the tears falling freely. I nodded toward her coat and she slowly opened it. Her chest was bare and bloody, the bastard had carved a message in her chest then seared the wounds closed with fire, the flesh blistered and blackened but still bleeding.

You're Next were the words carved there. I looked at

Nora and leaned forward and pulled the coat closed for her.

"He's gone insane," she rasped. "He beat Della then came at me, dragging me out of the house taking me to the place he called his pleasure den. I asked him why me and he told me he had a job for me then he… he said if I didn't do what he wanted me to…" She paused, taking in another heavy breath, and then let it out slow as she spoke.

"He's crazy…kept mumbling that he always got them to talk…always."

She let the words drop off then cried for a few minutes, her sobs more for what he had done to her than the pain he had caused her. I watched while she cried, a slow boil building in me. Nora may have been a kinky woman but she was still a woman and the damage Striker had done to her flesh, even if it could be repaired, would stay with her for the rest of her life.

"Stay here." I stood and motioned to the other attendants who stood at the bottom of the stairs. I stepped in and asked one more question of her before they came into the room. "This place he took you too, do you know where it is?"

"Downtown." she sniffed. "An old warehouse downtown."

"Can you give me anything more specific?"

"I could see the Heer's building from the windows up high before he took me down into the basement." She let out a gasp and clutched her chest, the attendants hovering over her and waving me out of the way.

Blood came from the corner of her mouth as her eyes rolled up showing me the whites for a moment then rolled back.

"I could smell old paper and machine oil," she gasped just before she passed out, the attendants loading her on the gurney and ushering her down the stairs.

****

Shelly had a broken leg, a broken wrist and a concussion. The doctors told me she would be fine, just off her feet for a couple of months. Nora was another story. The message carved on her chest was deep and there were second and third degree burns on top of it. She could be fixed but she would still have scars. She also had a bad heart from birth. Her heart skipped a beat the doctor told me. It had stopped a couple of times while she was being tortured. Whoever the torturer was had brought her back, looking like he had used electricity to jump start her heart, a couple of the burn marks indicating this.

Pat gave me the once over so after I had answered all his questions he turned me loose to head back to Shelly's room. My kitten was asleep, her right leg in a cast along with her arm and a bandage around her head where she had a cut from the fall. I eased up on the bed and looked at her for a few moments, cursing Striker which stepped the boil up in me another notch.

He had sent Nora knowing that when we saw what kind of shape she was in, Shelly or me would try to help her and once one of us was in her sights, Nora would get one and he would do the other with his knife throwing trick. He had failed on both counts, but there was something else Striker was holding over Nora, one of the attendants telling me she was mumbling a name over and over as they worked on her and I was gonna find out what that was as soon as I could talk to her. Right now Shelly was my main concern.

A while back we had talked marriage and both of us decided maybe we should wait a little while. But after this, I don't think waiting is gonna be an option. Pat came in as I was still thinking and stood for a few moments, his hat in his hands.

"Is she gonna be okay?" he asked me.

"Yeah." I brushed a lock of hair off her forehead. "Did

you talk with Vicky?"

"I did, she said Striker told her she was his plaything, his stress reliever, nothing more," Pat told me, "He kept her prisoner in her own bedroom."

"He sent Nora as a warning." I turned toward him, slid off the edge of the bed and led him out in the hall.

"Yeah, I had a little talk with Nora after they got done with her, she said you were to blame for Striker doing what he did to her." Pat shook his head. "All the while he was carving his warning in her chest he told her you were to blame. He took away her beauty so she was gonna take something away from you because you forced him to do what he had to do and if she didn't do what he told her to, her daughter would be the next to feel his blade."

A daughter, the bastard was beyond taking alive as far as I was concerned.

"Have you contacted the daughter?" My voice was low as I spoke to him.

"Uh-huh, she's in protective custody until we catch the son of a bitch"

"Good, did she tell you Striker took her to a warehouse downtown, one that she could see the Heer's building from. She also told me the place smelled like old paper and machine oil."

"There's an old warehouse on the north side of St. Louis Street, used to be leased by the newspaper to store their paper in and some of the old presses they used to use. She might be talking about that one. I'll get some men and we'll check it out." Pat tossed his hat on and headed for the door.

I nodded as he left, waited a few minutes then slapped on my hat and headed out the door, kissed Shelly plus told the nurse to take good care of her.

This was the second time Shelly had been put in the hospital because of some maniac I had been after. We have always known there was a risk but Shelly always told me that if I was gonna play with the bad guys she had to expect it. This time though she could have gotten killed and if that had happened nothing would have kept me from putting a bullet in Striker then ripping his head off and taking it to Biscayne, even if Pat and his boys were watching.

Of course I was gonna put a bullet in his head anyway, the ripping off his head just the mad talking. I cut over onto Booneville Avenue then up to St. Louis Street, pulled into the lot by the old warehouse and parked. I sat for a few minutes then crawled out and headed toward the front of the building. It would take Pat at least an hour to pull everybody in he was gonna use to search the warehouse, I wanted to search it before he got there, maybe find Striker and make a lead anchor out of him.

I tried the front door and it was locked, my foot doing the unlocking. I pulled a penlight out of my coat pocket and flipped it on, the thin beam lighting the way in front of me enough so that I wouldn't trip over something. Trash littered this room, a lot of wine bottles and cigarette butts littered the floor. Some of the crates that were stacked about had been broken apart and used as firewood, the remnants of a fire lying in the middle of the room's floor.

On the north wall a metal sliding door was part way open so I squeezed through, my light found more crates, old printing equipment and a couple of rolls of paper, half of it gone. It's a wonder the winos hadn't burned the place down lighting fires in here, the paper old and brittle, tinder for a match. I walked on, reached the back wall and a staircase going down. I eased down the stairs, feeling each one out as I went, making sure none of them snapped and none of them creaked as I made my way down.

In the basement, old rolls of newsprint were stacked against the walls on metal racks, the rolls held in place by steel rods that looked rusty and ready to snap in two. I eased my way down the aisle between them, stopped and listened ever so often to see if anyone might be in the room.

I moved on, flashed my light between the stacks of paper, nothing showing but the occasional rat.

About halfway into the room I stopped, the sound of footsteps thumping the floor ahead of me along with the sound of liquid spilling on the floor. I flipped off my light and slipped up next to a rack of paper, the smell of kerosene filling my nose along with the soft sound of someone muttering loud in the still air. I peeked around the rolls and saw Striker slosh kerosene on the paper and on a couple of metal tables in the cleared area in the room. Striker was still dressed in the hospital gown, the front of it splattered with blood. Once the can was empty, he gave it a toss, the can clattering and banging loud in the stillness.

Then he stripped off the gown right down to his underwear, tossing them on the table in front of him. He paused a moment, touched the bandage on his jaw and swore. I eased around the corner some more as Striker turned his back to me, his head tilted up, his arm raised, a sliver of metal flashing in the lights.

"One last chance," his voice silky with a slight rasp to it, you could hear the death's head grin in it. "Where is the notebook?"

There was a silence as Striker took a step forward, his arm drawing back then shooting out, a dull thud sounding in the quiet, someone screamed as he reached over and picked up another knife from the table. I tried to move to get a better look at who he was tossing knives at but would have to step out in the open so I stayed where I was and listened.

"Vell," he shrugged his shoulders, "maybe the woman knows. I don't think she will be as stubborn as you. I know she won't be as stubborn to the pain and let's be honest, women are screamers and Mien Gott do I love to hear them scream."

There was joy in his voice when he said this, like a little kid looking forward to getting a candy sucker or comic book. I stepped out from behind the rolls of paper, cleared my throat as Striker turned. I fired as he dove toward the table, knocking it over, the slug hit the metal top and sparked, the kerosene flaming up fast, Striker screamed as he came to his feet, his undershirt on fire along with the bandage on his face.

He beat them out as he ran, the son of a bitch was fast, ducking between some paper rolls as I pulled off two more shots, both doing nothing more than kicking up paper off the rolls. I looked across the flames and saw a man shackled to a floor beam, his toes scraping the floor. I ran through the fire to him, stepped back and fired at the chain holding him to the beam, he dropped to a heap on the floor as I grabbed him up and dragged him across the floor the way I came, the fire having caught the spools of paper on fire and spreading.

He came to as I got to the steps, I asked him if he could walk and he nodded. We staggered up the steps, smoke filling the open stairway in thick, black clouds. I was halfway across the upstairs room when I heard Pat yell. I yelled back, he and a couple of uniforms came running up. The uniforms took the man as Pat and I ran out behind them, the floor already falling through in spots.

"Was Striker in there," he yelled over the roar of the flames.

"Yeah." I coughed a little, wiping at my eyes stinging from the smoke. "I took a shot at him but he dived behind a metal table, the slug sparked the kerosene he had poured around on the floor."

"Kerosene? He was gonna burn the place down?"

"Yeah, with this guy in it." I jerked my thumb at the guy the uniforms were lowering to the sidewalk.

"Who the hell is he anyway?"

Pat jerked his head toward the man as I answered, "My guess is Ralph. Shall we find out?"

Both Pat and I walked over to where one of the

uniforms were knelt beside him, his face swollen, only slits for eyes showed that he was still conscious. His clothes were in tatters, cut, bloodied and burned, a thin shiv stuck out of his leg. The uniform stood as we knelt down beside him. I took a cigar out and lit it. Pat grunted and asked if I didn't have enough smoke for one day. I told him it was a different kind of smoke as I shook his the man's shoulder and said in a loud voice, "Hey Ralph!"

Ralph groaned and jerked his head toward me as I leaned down closer. He looked at me through the slits in his face, his mouth moved but only grunts came out.

"Where's Monica, Ralph?" He did a sort of half assed shrug then mumbled something through his battered lips or tried to.

"Was she in the building?" Pat asked him. He shook his head no then groaned loud, a couple of ambulance attendants muscled in told us to get back. We did, the two of them checked him over then loaded him on the gurney and hauled him away.

"Well, I guess we'll just have to wait until he is in a room to talk to him." I turned around toward the fire, number two crew and number one crew hosing the building down around the flaming structure more than at it. They didn't want another fire like they had back in the 1900's which had burnt most of the square to the ground.

"You hoping he was still in there?" Pat stepped up beside me, the roar of the fire made us yell to be heard.

"Yeah, but I doubt it, the guy is like a cat if you know what I mean." One of the walls fell in shooting flames, smoke and hot ash shot into the air. "He's probably a little crispy though, when he dived behind the table he wallowed in the kerosene and lit up."

"Yeah?" Pat had a small smile on his face as we stepped back a little ways, the heat from the fire, even though it was just a little over twelve degrees outside still making it unbearable. In my gut I knew Striker had escaped the devil's claw. Guy's like him never die until old scratch decides it's their time and that time was close.

****

Shelly was awake and grumbling, bitching about not being able to go to the bathroom by herself and having to use a bedpan. I tried to keep a straight face but failed miserably and she cussed me. When the girl is mad she has a vocabulary that is only second to a sailor's, some of the words she used even burning my ears.

Pat leaned in the door and asked if he could talk to me for a minute. Shelly grunted another blue word and I patted her arm, telling her while I was out I was gonna acquire a bar of soap to clean up her speech. That sent her off again as I stepped out and closed the door.

"Man." Pat smiled from ear to ear. "She does have a temper."

"With a mouth to match. What's up?"

"We had a little talk with Ralph." Pat leaned against the wall and tipped his fedora back. "He said Monica was the one who had burned the face off the guy. He told me he had left her there to see a guy about a gun, he was gone a few hours and when he came back noticed there was a lot of black smoke rolling out the chimney. He said he rushed into the house and there was Monica, parked in a big easy chair, her eyes wide and wild, the fire blazing high, the guy's head in the fireplace, Monica having piled dry wood on top of the head. She also held a twenty-two pistol in her hand.

"He said he put the fire out with water then went outside, the smell making him lose his lunch. Monica never moved. Once he got a grip on his stomach he went back inside and asked Monica where she got the gun. She told him he had it, pointing at the charred head in the fireplace. She thought it was Striker at first then when she saw he wasn't cut on his face, she figured it was one of Russo's men sneaking in the back door. She hid in the bedroom with a poker and when he got into the living room, she waylaid him, tied him up and after that she didn't remember much until she saw him in the fireplace, so they packed what they could and got the hell out of there."

"So she was the one who shot him in the head?"

"Yeah, but she doesn't remember doing it least that's what she told Ralph."

"You tell him who it was?"

"Yeah, and he started to cry. He said Monica had changed, you could see it in her eyes. Especially after she had seen what had happened to her sister in the bedroom."

"So it was her who came back."

"Yeah, she figured Mona had chickened out and went back for a key and the jewels. She tried to pawn them but found out they were paste so she contacted Ralph and begged him to help her."

"Did he ask her what the key was for?"

"He did, but she just told him it was her ticket out of this hick town and his too if he wanted it."

It was the same old spiel…money…coinage…the dream of not having to worry anymore about bills and having everything one could ever want. Oh, they might get away, live it up for a while but when they weren't looking, they would drop the hammer on them and whatever they had left would buy their tombstones.

"How did Striker find them?" I asked.

"Probably through Biscayne's people."

I nodded and turned back toward Shelly's room, stopped then looked over my shoulder at Pat.

"Meet me at Benny's this evening around seven." I opened the door and stepped back inside before Pat could ask why.

****

The cold was keeping a lot of people at home; Benny's only having four customers this evening. Of course Stella was working, her uniform a little tighter, her cleavage a little deeper. She told me she was sorry to hear about Shelly then said if I needed anything to let her know then she winked at me, turned and walked away, her hips doing a sway that was intentional. I chuckled and sipped at the coffee I had ordered, Stella taking longer to pour it than usual.

If I was one of those fictional PIs I would tap that, but fiction and real life are entirely different. The fictional PI with a girlfriend might get away with it but in real life, especially in this town, Shelly would get wind of it and I would lose the one thing I care for which is why I stay on the up and up. I love Shelly too much to do that to her but a guy can dream can't he?

It was a little after seven when Pat came in, the sun had already gone down and only a couple of people remained in the diner. Pat was bundled up good, his scarf wrapped around his mouth and his hat pulled down low over his eyes to cut the wind. He looked like one of those mystery men in the magazines, face hidden, only his eyes showing. He unbuttoned his coat, took off the scarf and tipped his hat back as he sat down and peeled off his gloves. Stella came up and Pat ordered coffee, then turned to me, Stella looking a little hurt, a pout formed on her lips as she walked away.

"You ain't making any points there buddy." I nodded toward Stella as she walked away.

"What the hell are you talking about?" He looked over his shoulder then back at me, his face flushed as he growled in a low voice, "Don't start."

"Hey, she could be a real stress reliever." I cocked an eye at him.

"So why am I here?" Pat grunted at me changing the subject.

"Monica and the key she went after."

"What about it?"

"Mason made the key for her."

"And you've known this for how long?" He had on his cop face, his brow furrowed and his eyes narrowed.

"A few days." I shrugged. Pat cussed under his breath and leaned back in his chair shaking his head. After a few minutes he leaned forward, the frown on his face relaxing a bit.

"So what's the key to?"

"My guess is a safety deposit box, I have a good guess where it is and before you demand to know where, I'm still working on that." Pat gave me a hard stare and grunted as I sipped my coffee. He knew I had already figured out where it was but knew to press me would only get him half assed answers and nothing more.

He started to speak when Stella came back with his coffee, poured it slow and asked him if he wanted anything else, a sensual smile on her lips. Pat told her no and she hesitated for a moment, then pouted again and walked away.

"I think she likes you." I chuckled.

"Don't." Pat dumped some sugar in his coffee then stirred it as he asked, "So this notebook, it has some damning evidence in it?"

"So I'm told it seems our illustrious D.A. is listed in it."

"Really?" The shocked look on Pat's face was classic and I laughed.

"Uh-huh, not for taking pay-offs or anything like that. Seems he has a taste for the seedier side of life."

"Okay, so some of those nights he spent working late was a different kind of work?"

"Exactly."

"What about Della. How does she figure into this?"

"Striker is a deviant, pain is his thing, it gets him off.

Of course she turned him away and that didn't set too well with him. I suspect he was looking for a place to hide out."

"Uh-huh," Pat said as he sipped the Joe and made a face.

"Della might be into the dark side of life but when it comes to guys like Striker, well, she knows her limits plus she didn't want a crazy causing her any trouble."

"So tell me, you got any clue where this notebook might be?" He cocked a questioning eye at me and waited.

I smiled at him but didn't say a word, just sipped my coffee again and shrugged.

Pat leaned back in his chair and sighed. This whole case depended on the notebook and Monica. Hell, it was the lead to Pat's investigation as well as mine and I was holding back on him. He could have taken me downtown, grilled me and if I didn't tell him what he wanted to know, lock me up until I did. But he also knew it would do no good because he would have to let me go then he would get nothing but dead bodies plus no notebook.

"Wellman is gonna chew my ass but okay, just keep me informed and watch your ass," Pat took another sip of coffee then stood.

"Leaving so soon?" I asked.

"Yeah, and if you know what's good for you, you will too." He dropped a quarter on the table and started bundling up again. Stella gave him a smile and a wave, Pat nodding as he left. She came back to the table, picked up his cup, asked if I needed a refill and I told her no as I stood, dropped a quarter tip on the table and walked toward the front. Benny waved me off as I dug in my pocket to pay for the coffee so I thanked him and exited the diner, Stella watching me. She winked at me as I passed the front window, pushed her sweater puppies out against the uniform blouse, two nubs showing through the cloth which made me wish Shelly was back home.

As I stepped out the door I pulled the belt on my coat

tight and flipped the collar up against the cold. Pat didn't realize it but the reason Wellman was riding his ass was because he knew about the notebook, probably heard about it from Paton who undoubtedly was told by Russo to lean on Wellman to get it back. I figure this was why he tried to arrest me at the hospital, taking me to the Station the farthest thing from his mind. He hadn't counted on Pat showing up, he figured his boss had gone home and if I disappeared, Paton would probably claim that Striker had nabbed me which might have been a true statement if Striker had paid them to get me outside. I guess I have an angel who looked over me.

I crossed the street and made my way toward Kelso's to have Fisk put the word out to find Monica. I was halfway there when a black Chevy four door pulled up; two goons crawled out walked toward me. My hand dipped under my coat and they stopped, both of them held up their hands, palms forward as they eased toward me some more.

"Mr. Russo would like to speak to you," one of them said his hands not as high as the other ones.

"What about?" I asked, my hand stayed where it was.

"A certain article I have lost possession of," a voice spoke from inside the car. "No tricks Mr. Black, at least not from my people."

I stepped off the curb, my hand came part way out of my coat but stayed close enough to grab my pistola if I needed to. I crawled into the back and sat down. The two goons crawled in front, the last one in shut the back door before he crawled in the seat.

Frank "The Fat man" Russo was nothing like Sampson. Frankie is a short, fat man, with three chins, flabby cheeks and piggish eyes. His suits were tailor made; I figured the guy who turned them out for him probably made a fortune in just the cloth alone. Today he had on a dark gray suit which made him look fatter and wore a dark gray fedora cocked to the left side of his head. A silver tipped cane sat between his legs, his hands resting on the knob, one on top of the other. I had heard there was a gun encased in the cane, the press of a button under the knob releasing the trigger for its use.

Frankie shifted toward me, the seat springs screamed and the car leaned a little to the left.

"I have a proposition for you," Frankie spoke, his eyes narrowed a little, a cold smile crossed his lips "One that will benefit the both of us."

"And that is?" I asked as I leaned my back against the door, my right elbow found the door handle just in case.

"A certain item was stolen from me," his voice was nasal, like he was talking out of his nose without moving his lips. "That item I would like to have back before it falls into unsavory hands. I am offering you one hundred thousand for the return of said item."

"And what makes you think I have it?" His smile widened his eyes cold and hard.

"My dear Max," his voice held a hard edge to it, "I never said you had it. I want you to find it and return it to me."

"For one hundred thousand, huh?" I arched one eyebrow as I answered him.

"That is correct," Frankie said.

"And if I refuse?"

"That would not be a wise thing to do." The smile turned nasty as he spoke.

Most guys would have given the offer some serious thought, but I'm not most guys. This notebook had brought in a maniac and a lot of dead bodies were attributed to persons trying to find it. One of them being an innocent which had gotten my ire up from the minute I saw her carved up like a Christmas turkey.

"Why don't you offer the one who stole it from you the money?" I asked him.

"I have," Frankie grunted, "but they are greedy, their

price is half a million or they will turn it over to the D.A."

"Let me think about it," I said as we pulled back up in front of my office after going around the block.

"I see, well, when should I expect an answer?" Frankie asked.

"I'll let you know." I opened the car door and stepped out, slammed it as I stepped up on the curb, my hand deep under my coat gripping the butt of my .45 as the car pulled away and turned onto Jefferson then disappeared.

CHAPTER 15

I figured Russo would show up sooner or later. I mean, he has a lot riding on that notebook, mostly whether he spends time in the pen or back in the rackets. If I had it my way he would spend time in the pen, but that ain't gonna happen unless I get a handle on Monica before he does. I turned my coat collar up and headed toward Kelso's again, the darkness cold and black, the wind still whipping down Commercial Street with a vengeance.

The weather man said it was supposed to be the coldest night on record, the thermometer already reading four below. As I hustled toward Kelso's, a couple of winos hustled by me, both of them wrapped in layers of clothes, their breaths plumed out in foggy streams as they picked up speed toward the mission, hoping to make it on time to find a good spot to bed down. On nights like this, the mission was packed wall to wall. Father Masters told me one time if he could stack them like cord wood the cops would find less wino-icicles the morning after.

Kelso's was about as dead as Benny's, but not quite. No matter what the weather, be it blazing hot or freezing cold there are people who decide they need a drink. Of course Fisk isn't one of them, his position at Kelso's is warming the booth he calls his office. I slid in across from him and he looked up at me, a big smile on his face as he shook his head.

"Jerry was in here a few minutes ago telling me this crazy story about seeing you crawl into Russo's car," Fisk chuckled.

"Did he now?"

"Uh-huh, said we should all take off our hats and say a silent prayer for Max Black, raise a drink to him as this was surly his last ride." A grin turned up the corners of his mouth and I laughed then looked over at the bar, Jerry lying on the floor down at the end, a bottle in his hand, a smile on his face.

"He's an eloquent man." Fisk looked also. "So eloquent Kelso just gave him the bottle and told him to enjoy."

"Sorry I missed it."

"Yeah." Fisk leaned on the table his eyes narrowing. "So did Russo want you to get his notebook for him?"

"Yes he did."

"How much?"

"One hundred thousand."

Fisk let out a low whistle as he sat back.

"Are you going to do it?"

"I told him I'd think about it. Any news on Monica?" I changed the subject. Fisk knew me well enough to know what the answer was.

Fisk leaned forward again; his voice low as he spoke. "Rumor is that she is hiding out with a male friend, one John Harmon. Rumor also is that he put her up to it, planned the whole thing so he could get the notebook to make a deal."

"What kind of deal?"

"Well, one was to clear up Monica's gambling debt

and before you cut in, yes, she was in debt up to her nipples. Harmon then wanted a percentage of the prostitution racket, fifteen percent which would put him in the money until Bruce confronted him and took him out. Monica told Bruce the whole story and Bruce thought it was a swell idea."

"You mean to tell me Bruce whacked him?" A shocked look crossed my face.

"No, took him out." Fisk laughed. "It's said Harmon came to work a few days later with a fat lip and a couple of shiners."

I shook my head and leaned back in the seat. Fisk nodded as he continued.

"Harmon *was* stepping out with Monica, you just didn't know it because one of them would leave by the back entrance and the other the front," I made a face, Fisk nodded again.

"Yeah, there is a back way out of the restaurant, the door set in the wall, bricked over, the inside door a heavy metal job with a steel lever holding it shut. You have to look real close to see where it is, a hallway leading to it where the back rooms are. You can't see them from the gaming room either, one of Russo's hoods takes you around the corner of the room where there is a little alcove, knocks three time and the wall opens up for entry. One of the rooms is used to count the take after the night is done."

"So how did Monica get hold of the book?" I leaned in closer; Fisk looked at me with his dark eyes and smiled.

"All the tallies were written down at the end of the night in a ledger, Russo taking the tally sheets and seeing to it himself. The notebook was back there also. After the ledger was finished, Russo jotted down what was owed to him by certain high officials, also what whore they spent the most time with that night or went home with. Seems there was a disturbance out in the main room one night. One that had to have his attention so when he went to take care of it, Monica had hid out in one of the rooms, snuck out, grabbed the notebook and slipped out the back door."

"Making Russo look like a fool." I chuckled.

"Yeah, a big one," Fisk agreed. "Which is why he probably made you the offer, he knows you Max, he knows either hell or high water you'll acquire the book one way or the other."

I stood, palmed off the usual fiver to Fisk and headed toward the door, watched the bar as I left just in case another of Russo's boys was on watch.

****

I walked back to the office and opened the door, stepped in and flicked on the light, walked to Shelly's desk and picked up the phone to call the hospital. They rang Shelly's room for me and I told her I would be by in a bit to see her. She told me to bring her something to eat, the god awful food they served here made her want to puke. I laughed and asked her what she wanted? She told me her to bring her chocolates, the kind with the cherry centers. I said I would and hung up just as a draft of cold air hit my back. As I turned around, the muzzle of a .22 caliber pop gun pointed at my eye, the woman behind it shaking.

Monica Stedman was wild eyed and pale faced, the coat she wore covered in mud with something that looked like soot smudging it also. The hand she had the .22 in shook so hard all I would have had to do was duck, grab her hand a take it away from her. She then did the unexpected, stepped forward and shoved the heater closer to my face as she licked her lips to speak.

"I know what you want and you can't have it!" Her voice was low, a slight tremble to it.

"And why not?" They were right, she smelled delightful.

She didn't expect that answer and it rattled her, rattled

her enough that she lowered the .22 for a second and I grabbed her wrist, her fingers jerking, a pea sized piece of lead hit the wall to my left gouging out a piece of plaster. I wrenched it from her hand and she yelled, her hand holding the purse slammed me upside the head. Whatever she had in it was heavy, hard enough to have me seeing stars for a second, but only for a second, not enough of them for her to get away.

She started to bolt, my foot going out catching her leg, Monica going for the new window in the door head first. I grabbed her coat collar and stopped her, pulled her back about a foot then dropped her on her face. She squealed and rolled over, her feet slammed out, one foot aimed for my knee and the other for the cajones. Neither made a connection. I grabbed her coat and jerked her up off the floor, the muzzle of my .45 stared her in the face.

"This .45 has a hair trigger so I wouldn't try kicking me again," I growled at her. Monica swallowed hard, her eyes glued to the hole in the end of the muzzle which probably looked like a cannon to her. I grabbed her by the arm and led her to the chair beside Shelly's desk, gave her a push so she plopped down in it. She was a redhead; her hair mussed and fell in waves down to her shoulders. I couldn't tell what was under the coat but I could imagine lots of curves, plus a high bust by the way they pushed against the coat. Her face was slightly long but in a pretty way, her nose small, her eyes a fiery green.

Like I said, her coat was dirty and one of her nylons was torn, the hole showing a firm calf pale and muscular. I sat down behind the desk, rested the butt of my .45 on the top and watched her as she held her hands clasp together. They were shaking.

"A lot of people are looking for you." Monica nodded her eyes not so wild now.

"Striker, Russo's boys, the police." I leaned on the desk, my .45 still aimed at her.

"And you," she snapped, her eyes blazing hotter.

"But I don't want you dead. Neither do the cops. All we want is the notebook."

A puzzled look came across her face as her eyes softened a little.

"You don't?" she asked, "But Harmon told me…"

I shook my head no and lowered the .45. So Harmon had fed her a line of bullshit to keep her in line.

"So Harmon was the master mind behind this?"

She nodded and said, "Harmon told me once we got the book we could start fleecing the big time names in it, Wellman being the first on the list. He also said you were tailing us, probably hired by Bruce and with your reputation possibly paid to rough him up a little to scare him off."

"Yeah, Bruce hired me Monica, but it was just to follow you to get pictures of you and Harmon together, nothing more. I guess he wasn't satisfied with what I got for him." I shook my head.

"He wasn't. He waited till Harmon got off of work and followed him back to his house and threatened Harmon with a gun. Bruce told me Harmon begged him not to shoot him, told him he had something that could make all three of us rich if Bruce would just listen to him. Bruce didn't shoot him just pistol whipped him and took the notebook. I was there at Harmon's house when he did it. I tried to stop him but Bruce pointed the gun at me and told me to stay back. You see, Harmon and I were getting ready to run away together.

"He was going to do the same to me until I told him about the notebook. He told me to hand it over and he wouldn't do to me what he did to Harmon. I gave it to him then he took me out to the car, told me if I said a word about this I would end up like Harmon, or worse."

Her tears were flowing freely now her makeup smeared and her lips trembling.

"While we drove back to our house he asked me about the notebook so I told him it was from Russo, it had a lot of important names in it of people in the city and Harmon and I were going to blackmail them. Once we got to the house, Bruce went through it then he said it was a good idea, then he left, a couple of hours later he came back and told me someone was following him and we needed to get out of the house fast. He went into the bedroom and told me to go out the back and get into the car, a few minutes later he came running out, the pistol in his hand firing at someone in the house. Bruce took off about the time two men came out the back, drove across the back yard and through the fence. They came after us but we lost them and went to my sisters."

"Question?" I stopped her before she could get going again. "How long did you and Bruce have the notebook?"

"A couple of weeks. Bruce ditched the Chevy we had, traded it to a farmer for a Buick then he contacted Russo and told him what it would take to get the notebook back."

"And did he agree?"

"I don't know, Bruce talked to him." Her voice cracked a little as she spoke. I leaned back in my chair and eyed her for a moment, then asked, "Did Ralph and Mona know what you two were up to?"

"Yes, they both did, Mona was the one who suggested she go back to the house and get me some clothes." Monica said as she sobbed into her hanky.

"Look Monica, I want to help..."

"You just want the notebook," she cut me off, a sneer on her lips.

"Uh-huh, I do but to draw out the bastard who killed your husband, your sister and your brother-in-law."

"But I killed a man," her voice soft as she looked at me. "I thought he was one of Russo's men trying to get the notebook but he wasn't, he was just a common burglar."

Tears were rolling from her eyes as she spoke, her

hanky a wet mess so I pushed the box of Kleenex toward her and she took one, dabbed at her eyes and sniffed.

"Where's the notebook Monica?" I asked. She looked up at me then reached in her purse and took out a key, laid it on the desk, her hands still shaking.

"Bruce took it," she told me, one finger still on the key. "I found the key on his key ring and made an impression of it then had that old man Mason make a copy of it. I believe it's to a safe deposit box."

"So the original key is on the key ring he has on him." I laughed. Bruce had the key on him while Striker was working him over and Bruce wouldn't talk. I slipped the key from under her finger and put it in my vest pocket and my .45 back in its home, picked up the phone and asked the operator to connect me with the Station. I asked for Pat. The desk sergeant told me he wasn't in but he would have the dispatcher get him on the radio. I told him I had Monica in in my office and if he wanted to question her to come on down.

As I hung up the phone the office door slammed open, the chatter of a Chicago typewriter filled the air over my head. I dove for the floor and grabbed my .45 again, Monica screamed as .45 slugs from the chatter box pounded the desk and floor around me. I heard someone yell, "It's the Stedman bitch, grab her" as I rolled toward Shelly's desk as lead stitched a path where I had been. I figured if this was it and I was going to go out I was gonna take at least one of them with me.

I put both feet against Shelly's desk and gave it a shove. The desk, mostly riddled with holes came up off the floor at the gunman. I heard the guy grunt and cuss as I stood up, the hood staggered back against the wall trying to aim. You know how they say that your life flashes before your eyes before you're about to bite it? Well, I never got the chance to find out.

The muzzle of the chatter gun was leveling toward me

and the hood's face had a big smile on it which suddenly disappeared in a spray of blood, bone and brains as I pulled the trigger. There was an exchange of gunfire outside, .38 slugs tossed one way and a .45 tossing them back. I came up off the floor and went to the doorway; a body hunkered down behind an old Ford as another car revved up and peeled rubber to get away. I slipped back in the doorway as the body moved toward me, stepping back a couple of paces just in case.

"Max, it's Pat Max!" Pat yelled as he came toward me and through the doorway, looking down at the body in front of him.

"Jesus, you are one lucky son of a bitch." Pat stepped over the body and walked toward me. He pointed to the tail of my trench coat I hadn't taken off yet. Between my legs were four bullet holes, two on the right side and two on the left.

"Yeah." I took the coat off and tossed it onto Shelly's office chair. Along with the coat, bullet holes scarred the wall behind the desk and the floor, her desk was riddled with them, her chair had two slats knocked out of the back and a couple slugs splintered the seat. Yeah, I had been damned lucky or the shooter wasn't any good at his job, I figured it was the latter.

With Pat I walked over to the hood slumped against the wall, a big hole in his head and one eye, his only eye, bugging. Then it hit me, where was Monica? I jumped over the body and onto the sidewalk, looking both ways then cussed.

"Where's Monica?" I whirled around as Pat came out behind me.

"Probably in the car that pulled away as soon as I pulled up," Pat said. "I had a choice and I figured the chatter gun was more important."

"Damn!" I shoved my .45 back home.

"Did you recognize the car?" I asked him pulling a

cigar out of my vest and looking it over. It was a little bent but would smoke.

"No, but one of the men who shoved her into it was Biscayne's man." Pat holstered his piece back under his coat and picked up the phone on the floor, inspecting it then dropping it. "Did she tell you anything?"

"Yeah, she did, she gave me something also." I motioned for him to follow me back in the office. Once there I pulled the key out of my vest pocket and showed it to him, Pat looking it over.

"Did she tell you what it went to?" Pat asked.

"A safe deposit box." I snatched the key back as he reached for it slipping it back in my pocket. Pat's eyes narrowed as he pointed at me.

"That's evidence," he growled at me.

"No, it's a bargaining chip," I growled back.

"Okay, explain?"

"When they find out Monica doesn't have the key they're going to come calling so when they do, I'll set up a meeting place of which you will be informed of, (which wasn't gonna happen). I have just one request though, let me handle the meeting, I'm sure it will be one of Biscayne's cohorts. I have another request also."

"You want Striker," Pat answered.

"Yeah I plan on making him hurt before I put one between his eyes." My voice was nasty as I said it. Pat stood quiet for a moment, his face a stony mask as he thought over what I had asked.

"Alright Max, but I want Striker alive, no bullet between the eyes, can you possibly do that?

"I'll see what I can do." My mouth twisted up in a nasty smile.

"I mean it Max." Pat pointed at me. "Well, alive enough to pay for what he has done."

Oh, I'll leave him alive enough for Pat to make a collar, that is, if Striker lets me leave him alive enough. Pat also had a bone to pick with the little shit, the wound in his shoulder being the main one but I couldn't guarantee anything and Pat knew it. He'd just have to take what I left him of Striker which might not be too much, head shots are always messy.

Pat went back out to his car and radioed in, telling them to send Ross and a couple of uniforms along with the lab boys. I went back into Shelly's office, picked up my trench and examined the holes, feeling a cold chill run down my back.

Yeah, I had been lucky. Even if the shooter was experienced, any one of the numerous slugs he had sprayed the room with could have put my lights out. Maybe I have a guardian angel looking over me or maybe the devil just isn't ready for my rebellious ass to drop in on him. Either way I figure this was about as close as I had come to biting it.

I went back in my office and hung the coat up on the coat rack behind my desk and pulled out my second trench, this one not as good as the other but just as warm. I slid into it then walked back out to where Pat stood shaking his head as he looked around. I asked him if he needed me for anything else. He grunted a no so I told him if he did, I would be at the hospital with Shelly. He nodded just as a car with four uniforms pulled to a halt at the curb, their siren blaring.

CHAPTER 16

Shelly was fit to be tied when I walked into her room. One of the nurses had come in and told her that she had heard on the radio that there had been a gun battle on Commercial Street, one man dead.

"Well it ain't me." I grinned and sat down on the side of the bed.

"Smart ass," she snapped at me, her eyes locked on mine. "Which side was it?"

"Biscayne's men." I shrugged. "Monica was there also, but Biscayne's people got her."

"And tried to get you," Shelly spoke in a low tone.

"Yeah, but they didn't, how are you doing?" I was glad I had changed trench coats.

"Don't change the subject, what did she tell you?"

I sighed and told her what Monica had told me then showed her the key. Shelly took it and looked it over, her face blank for a moment then a light bulb went off in her eyes.

"When we were kids, daddy had a safe deposit box in a bank. This looks like the key he had," she told me handing it back.

"That's what it's to kitten and I know which bank Stedman stashed the notebook in. All I need to do is get my friend Brad to let me look in it without getting Pat involved."

"Maybe Pat could help you…"

I cut her off and said, "Huh-uh, I want that notebook for leverage."

"No, you want it to draw Striker out."

"Damned right I do."

I slid the key back in my vest and told Shelly I would be right back and walked out to the nurse's desk to use the phone. Guess who was there? My favorite red head and she was just as nasty as ever, telling me to use a payphone, these were for hospital use only. I smiled at her and asked if she had taken an extra dose of mean ass pills today. She told me what she thought of me as I walked away, some of her words not very lady like.

I shoved a nickel in the slot then dialed the operator asking for the Station. The operator on the other end was my old friend Betty, the sexy voice with a body I had never seen.

"Hey sugar," she purred in a sultry tone, "I haven't talked to you in quite a while."

"Been kind of busy, so how you been?" I asked her.

"Lonely," she answered me then giggled.

If she had a body anything like the voice she shouldn't be.

"Listen, one of these days we need to get together for coffee," she said.

"Yeah, we can do that, just let me know when." It would never happen though; she would always be a voice with a body only to dream about.

"I'll do that, putting you through, bye."

There were a couple of clicks then Sargent Milton answered the phone. Milton was another one of the older men and I knew him well. He had been the beat cop for a while on Commercial Street until he got a bullet in his leg snapping a hamstring which chained him to a desk.

"Hey Milt, I need a favor?"

"Hello Max, what is it?"

"I need someone to stand at Shelly's door."

"You expect trouble?"

"Maybe, maybe not, I don't want to take any chances."

"Ok Max let me see what I can do."

I thanked him, hung up, then walked back to Shelly's room glancing over at the red head, the phone glued to her ear as she chatted with someone and laughed. Hospital use only I thought grinning as I stepped into Shelly's room, hearing the red head laugh. She sounded like a mule braying and I laughed out loud just before I closed the door, her head jerking around, her eyes drilling into me even through the door.

****

I was at Benny's the next day when a girl of about twenty slid in the booth across from me. She was a bottled blonde, her roots showing brown the tips of her hair frizzy. She had on heavy makeup, I figured to hide the wear and tear of her profession. She was dressed in a wool coat with a fur collar buttoned up tight around her neck. She had a pretty face even with the mileage, high cheek bones and a pert little nose. Her eyes were heavily made up, mascara thick and clumped, her blue-green eyes reflected the world she knew.

She opened her coat and she had on a silk blouse, the front cut low enough to show her deep cleavage, the swell of her breasts strained against the fabric. I lay my fork down, sat back in my seat and looked her in the eyes then asked, "What can I do for you sugar?"

"You have something Miss Biscayne wants," she

purred in a low voice. "She is prepared to negotiate terms on her acquiring it."

"Uh-huh," I grunted and shoved my plate away from me. "And how does she know I have it."

"She knows you have the key, once you find the notebook, she will negotiate for the book *and* Monica's life," the girl said.

"And if I refuse?" I stared at her, my eyes drilling into her. She began to sweat, beads of it rolled down her temples and cut tracks in the heavy makeup.

"Then Monica dies and so does your girlfriend." Her voice was shaky when she answered. I let a smile touch the corners of my mouth as I asked, "You're not used to making threats are you?"

"Look, I was just told to come here and tell you what I was told, they want an answer tonight." She swallowed hard and looked down at the table.

"How long do I have to find the notebook?" I asked still staring at her.

"When you have it you are to call this number." She looked up at me and handed me a slip of paper, her hand shook a little as I took it.

I let my smile widen to nasty as I looked at the paper, the blonde slid out of the booth and waited for an answer as she buttoned her coat back up. I nodded but as she started to turn to leave. I grabbed her wrist, gave it a squeeze and jerked her around, her eyes wide, a gasp coming out of her mouth.

"You tell Striker I have a bullet with his name on it," I hissed at her, the nasty smile still in place. "You tell him for me he is gonna die very badly. You tell him that, you understand?"

She gave a short nod then I let go, the girl rubbed her wrist as she walked out the door past the front windows and disappeared, a minute later a car drove past turning onto Booneville Street. I leaned back in my seat and tipped my hat back, unfolded the paper and read the number. It was bad enough Biscayne threatened to kill Monica if I didn't produce the book, but when she brought Shelly into it that was all it took.

I'd find the notebook alright but I didn't plan on letting her get her hands on it nor let Russo have it. I had another fellow in mind to turn the book over to and when I did, a lot of heads would roll around town, yes they would.

****

I remembered one time bumping into Bruce as he was coming out of the Union National Bank on the square, the same bank managed by Sammy boy. I had been up there seeing a client, a fellow who needed me to follow his wife, he suspected she was seeing a soldier boy on the side and he wanted proof before he cut her out of his will. I picked up the phone and had the operator connect me with Brad Morris, one of my poker buddies from way back, the same Brad who had the sniffles the last time I was there.

The phone rang three times and a woman answered so I asked if Brad was around. She said yes, he was but he was busy with a customer could he call me back? I said sure and gave her my number. I leaned back in my chair to wait. I had called Shelly earlier, the doctors telling her she might be able to go home in another week but she was to take it easy because she had a compound fracture, staying off her feet as much as possible. The doc even told her she could hire a nurse and gave her a couple of numbers to call.

I said that was a good idea then asked if the cop was still by her door? She said yes but before she could ask me anything about what was going on I told her I had to go, that I loved her then hung up. I hated doing that but she had enough to worry about without having to worry about me.

It was thirty minutes before Brad called me back, his voice raspy on the phone.

"Hey Max, been a long time buddy how are you?" he rasped then coughed away from the receiver.

"Yeah it has, you don't sound too good."

"I've got a damned cold." He stifled another cough. "I got it from my youngest daughter and she got it from school."

"Yeah, kids are good for that."

"Don't I know it. What can I do for you?"

"I need to know if Bruce Stedman had a safety deposit box there at the bank."

"Let me see I do believe he did have one here, let me check. Wasn't he the one they found in the alley a few weeks ago?"

"Yeah."

There was a pause for a moment, the sound of pages in a book turning.

"Yes, he did have one with us."

"Did his wife ever come down and see what was in it?"

"No, not that I know of. Is there anything I should be aware of?"

"No, the less you know the better off you'll be. This is between you and me okay?"

"Sure Max sure."

"Good, now I need a favor."

He knew what was coming; his voice lowered just a bit, "You need to get into it right?"

"Yeah, can you help me out?"

"You have the second key?"

"I do."

"Then come down a few minutes before closing."

"Thanks Brad."

"Yeah," Brad said and hung up.

Brad was taking a big chance letting me into the box, especially if his boss, you remember Sammy, found out that he had let me do it. I thought about calling Pat but that would only involve him and he would take the notebook and then bust the whole bunch which would get Monica and Shelly killed.

I stood and walked into the outer office, Shelly's desk already having been cleared out and taken to the dump, the holes in the floor and the wall reminding me of how lucky I had been.

I've have had a lot of close calls in the past and each time my friends had stepped in to keep me from walking up to St. Peter's Pearly Gates, that is if St Peter will have me. I could see myself standing in front of him, his wise eyes looking down on me, his head shaking no as I plead my case.

Oh I've killed a few people, but never have I killed them just for the sake of killing although it has crossed my mind a few times. The courts always deemed it self-defense although there were a few times it was questioned especially since Andy Russell, a reporter with the Leader gave me my motto. Good old Andy, the man is a pain in the ass but a good reporter.

I checked my watch, walked into my office grabbed my trench coat, slid into it then checked to make sure my .45 was ready just in case. I stood for a moment and watched the street, the cold north wind having let up, switched to the south and was whipping papers along with other debris across the icy patched street.

Even with all that had happened the city went on, even in the bitter cold it went on. These people were survivors. They withstood the hot summers, the bitter cold winters, the rationing and the blackouts that were a necessity with the war on. I've seen many a bald tire rolling down the street since new tires were a luxury and when they went bad, they walked. Yeah, good people but people who sometimes were led astray by those they trusted.

I opened the door and stepped out, locked it behind me and crossed the street to my old heap, once again checking it out just in case someone had visited it while it was inside.

I crawled in, checking the back seat first then cranked it over, the old Ford growling a couple of times then fired up.

When it got real cold the old lady sometimes just grunted and that was it. Maybe come spring I'll go down to Montgomery's to see if I can trade it in on a newer one, maybe a Tudor with a rumble seat. Shelly would like that I thought as I pulled out and headed toward the square.

CHAPTER 17

The Union National Bank is located on the south side of the square, really on the southeast corner if you want to get technical about it. The building is a two story stone structure with the bank below and offices rented out above, the upstairs offices' entrance to the right side of the building, the bank's entrance to the left.

As I rounded the pie in the center of the square, (for you newbies to Springfield, the pie is a big, round open spot in the center of the square where parking is when you can find it) and I got lucky, a parking space was open so I cut my wheels and slid into it, literally, a guy blasting his horn at me for beating him to it.

I crossed the street and stepped inside the bank, the feeling of stepping back in time hit you the minute you looked around. Most of the other banks had upgraded their teller's windows, opening them up by taking the bars down that were supposed to deter robbers from hopping over them and robbing them. It didn't so why have them.

Here the bars were still in place, the woodwork dark walnut polished to a soft gloss, the bars repainted black ever so often to keep up appearances. I started to take a step when a billy club thumped across my chest, the action made me jump and jerk my head to the right.

A guard stood there, a big fellow with a thick chest and burly arms, he wore a gray uniform that was spick and span and his shield clipped to his shirt was bright and shiny. He had a weathered face, his eyes in a permanent squint from too much sun, his nose big and flat, his lips thin, his chin marked with a scar.

"Say buddy," he stepped in close, "what's that bulge under your coat?"

I started to say something when out of the corner of my eye I saw Brad coming toward us, waving his hands and calling out to the guard.

"Buster," he said as he got closer. "He's okay Buster, he's a PI."

"A shamus huh?" Buster let out in a low growl.

"Yeah," I growled back at him. "Anything wrong with that?"

We both stared at each other for a few minutes then he shrugged, dropped the nightstick to his side but still stared. Brad grabbed me by the arm and pulled me toward the fence that separates the back from the front, Buster still drilling me. I could feel his eyes on my back as we went to Brad's desk.

Brad's desk was near the back west corner of the bank, a mahogany job piled up with files and ledger books. I grinned and sat down in the chair at the side of his desk, pulled out a cigar and offered it to him; he shook his head no so I clamped it between my teeth and fired it up.

"When did you guys get a guard," I asked him blowing smoke at the ceiling.

"A couple of weeks ago, the old man was told that soon his bank would receive some unwelcome visitors." Brad chuckled.

"Who told him that?" I laughed.

"Madam Tesco." Brad rolled his eyes and laughed with me. Madam Tesco was the premiere faker here in the city. She has many clients, most of them high city officials who take her predictions as gospel.

"That's where he's at this afternoon with his wife, getting a reading. It was the faker's suggestion he hire a guard to stand at the door to deter the robbers." Brad shook his head.

"From the looks of him he probably scares the customers more that he would a couple of bank robbers," I glanced over my shoulder at him and chuckled.

"So what's the deal with Stedman?" Brad leaned forward on his desk and spoke in a low voice.

"Like I told you, the less you know the better off you are."

He nodded and stood, motioned for me to follow him, the two of us heading to the vault. The vault was one of the older types, the door read Taylor, 1896 on the front. He took a ring of keys from his pocket and unlocked the bars just inside the mouth of the doorway. Once inside he stowed the key ring in his coat pocket then took out another key ring from the same pocket as he led me to a bank of safety deposit boxes on the south wall.

He pointed to the one that Stedman rented and I pulled out the key and handed it to him. Brad inserted both of them into the locks then turned them, opened the door and pulled out the metal box inside. He stepped over setting it on a table in the middle of the room then stepped back, his hands folded behind him.

I flipped the lid open and inside was the notebook. I picked it up and flipped through it, smiling as I read the names listed in it, most of them people I knew, their names listed in alphabetical order, how much they owed to Russo plus what preference of women they liked hanging on their arms.

I thumbed through some pages until I came to

Wellman's name and chuckled. Seems he's into Russo for around a thousand, he's partial to blondes, busty blondes the notation said. I stuffed the notebook in my coat pocket, flipped the box shut then handed it back to Brad.

"Keep this on the QT," I said as he slid the box back locking the door after I handed him the key.

"Keep what on the QT?" He grinned at me as he handed me back the key. I nodded, told him I would see him around then walked out of the vault to the front door, Butch giving me a nasty look as I walked out. I would keep the guy filed away in the back of my mind because something didn't feel right about him, something that smelled of hood but right now I had other things to worry about namely Monica and Shelly, plus how I was gonna keep the notebook out of the hoods' hands and get away with my hide intact.

Yeah, a lot to worry about but I had a plan; it just hasn't formed fully in my head yet.

****

I called the number the blonde gave me and guess what, The Bitch herself answered. Myra Biscayne comes from New Orleans and still would have been there if it hadn't of been for a certain District Attorney suddenly passing under suspicious circumstances. It seems this D.A. wanted to close Biscayne down also, but suddenly developed a case of lead poisoning, said lead poisoning led back to a friend of hers who sung like a bird when he was caught then died in his cell from a bad batch of gumbo before he could testify.

Suddenly, Biscayne found herself under the gun, the new D.A., a tea totaling, bible thumping maniac, or that was how he presented himself to the public, who was also a good friend to the dead D.A., decided Biscayne needed to be eliminated from this God fearing town. So he made a deal with the big boys in the town, take out Biscayne and they would receive leniency in certain matters when they came to the courts, which was a lie. Two attempts to take her out caused her to abandon the good old south and migrate up here where she set up business on her own with the help of certain known underworld backers, the last one being Russo himself.

Of course this was a rocky business partnership from the start, Biscayne always having run things her way when she was down south but this wasn't the south and Russo had a set way of doing things especially when it was getting his cut of the money of which Biscayne paid him when she felt like it, then it wasn't the agreed upon amount. Since then she has had a few dust ups with Russo, but nothing serious. They were supposed to be in a truce until things were settled but I'm sure that will change if Biscayne gets the notebook.

Biscayne told me that it was a good thing I had the book, that Monica was fine even though Striker had did a little work on her to tell him who she had given the key to.

"So where do you want to meet?" I grunted at her over the phone.

"My, my, such a nasty tone of voice Mr. Black. Surely you won't be this way when we do meet?" Her voice was sarcastic.

"Where?" I tried to cull some of the nasty out of my voice.

"Much better but not a lot." Biscayne chuckled. "You go to the Stedman house at midnight, Striker, Monica and a couple of my men will be there to greet you. In fact, Striker is very excited to meet you."

"Yeah, I'll bet, and then?" I let the nasty creep back in.

"They will release Monica and you will be escorted back here to hand me the ledger in person." Her voice had a touch of nasty now, the kind of nasty that means things could get bad.

"How do I know Striker will keep his hands and his blades to himself?" I growled at her into the receiver.

"Oh, don't worry *Mon Ami*, he will behave himself, Pierre will see to that. Until then love." Her voice was deadly sweet as she clicked off, the dial tone humming in my ear. Okay, so Striker was gonna be there probably with a knife to Monica's throat. I leaned back in my chair and mulled over what I was gonna do to take out three guys, and get Monica out before the maniac slit her throat. An idea came to mind but I didn't know if I could get what I wanted before midnight.

I grabbed up the phone to make a call, the phone ringing a dozen times before someone answered. The voice was raspy, a couple of coughing fits happened before it came back on line.

"Willy, this is Max," I said once the man on the other end asked what the hell I wanted.

"I need to see you Willy," I said.

"When?"

"Tonight."

"Geez man, I'm kinda busy."

"Well get unbusy. I'll be right over." I hung up the phone, Willy still babbling as my receiver hit the cradle.

Willy was a specialty man, if you needed something special for a job he could get it--at a price. His house was on the west side of town, just on the edge of the city limits, a big old two story farm house he had picked up back during the depression. From the outside, the old house looked just like that, an old house, the outsides weathered, paint peeling and clapboards warped. The old porch was just as weathered but sturdy, the front door looking as if a gust of wind would take it off its hinges.

But as they say in the detective magazines, looks are deceiving. The front door may have looked like bad wood but it was steel painted to look like bad wood, and if you looked real close, a thin wire ran around the frame making contact with the door itself. All a fellow had to do was grab the door knob of which he'll suddenly find himself flat on his back seeing stars, the doorknob wired for 120 volts.

All the windows were fixed the same plus the cellar door was rigged with a dynamite charge that would send whoever opened it to hell. So how do you get in? On the right side of the door was a little plate painted to look like the wood, just a touch and somewhere in the house a buzzer went off. I pushed it then five minutes later I pushed it again and was about to do it over and over when the front door opened, a mad Willy standing in the doorway in his underwear.

"Damn it Max," he snarled at me, "what the hell do you want?"

"First of all," I grinned as I pushed past him, "you need to get decent and second, I need some things."

It was then that he realized he was half naked and tenting. I laughed when he covered himself up and in a crouch headed toward the bedroom on his right. I guess he was busy. As I waited I walked on into the front room and as I did I spotted the busy he was at. A brunette lay on the couch, naked and stretching as she looked up at me and grinned. She was a full figured gal with full hips, a small waist and boobs that would make a priest's mouth water. As she sat up on the couch, her breasts rose big and firm, the nipples erect looking as if they could poke an eye out if you got too close.

She had a sensual face with a cute nose and chin, her lips full and kissable. Her eyes were charged with a sexual desire that makes old Pete jump a little when she looks at you. Her hair was a little mussed but it was long and thick and fell in waves and curls to her shoulders.

"Hi," she giggled, "my name is Clare."

"Max Black." I smiled and tried not to stare but it was damned hard.

"Nice to meet you Mr. Black. Did you come to party

with us?" Her voice dripped sex, the tip of her tongue flicked out and wet those delectable lips.

"No he didn't," Willy growled as he walked up behind me.

"Too bad." Clare stood and stretched again, her flesh rippled with each stretch. "I'll be in the bedroom if you change your mind."

She walked past me and Willy, the faint smell of honeysuckle touched my nose as one finger ran under my chin, her eyes told me I didn't know what I was missing.

"Nice huh?" Willy said his eyes in the same place mine was. "So what do you want?"

"I need some gas." I cleared my throat, wiping the image of Clare from my mind which was also damned hard to do.

"What kind?" Willy asked.

"The tear gas kind, in the grenades, not the shells."

"Okay, anything else?"

I looked at him and he chuckled. Usually he hem haws around when you tell him what you want and it surprised me that he didn't but would you if someone like her waited in the wings.

"Look, I heard all about what is going on, the word is you're gonna make a really bad man pay the price so I ask again, anything else?"

"What would you suggest?"

Willy rubbed his chin for a moment then smiled.

"Follow me."

We went through the living room into the kitchen, the smell of old grease and burnt food scented the air. Dishes were piled in the sink, some of them sporting a growth of mold that would make Sauk proud. From his pocket he took out a key, unlocked the cellar door then unhooked a wire as he pulled it part way open.

"You can't be too careful." Willie pointed to the inside of the doorway as we stepped onto the small landing, two sticks of dynamite secured to the inside two by four on the outer wall, a switch hooked to the wire, the minute the door was opened, the wire pulled and boom.

We went down the stairs, Willie turned on the lights as he went, the bulbs lighting the cellar's contents. Usually if I need something from Willy, he already has it upstairs. This was the first time I had been down into his storage room.

Racks of rifles lined one wall, from simple .22s to sniper rifles with scopes. Another rack held Thompsons, probably around ten in all and below them were other types of automatic machine guns, mostly Russian and English, well-oiled and ready. Crates of grenades and ammunition were stacked along another wall, beside the stack of crates four boards with pegs held pistols of various calibers on them.

In the middle of the room was a table on which lay two trench guns but not like the trench guns one would see used by the hoods. These were modified double barrels, the stocks sawed off into a pistol grip, the barrels cut down to the front grip. Willy picked one up and held it out to me, a grin on his face.

"This baby is lethal at close range but it kicks like a mule," he said as I looked it over.

"Is it a twelve?" I asked him.

"Uh-huh, I call it the Ball Buster." His grin widened to a smile, "I even have a holster for it."

He stepped over to a cabinet and opened it up, pulled out a leather rig with a long belt attached; the double barreled pistol fit it like a glove.

"Usually you wear it looped over your shoulder, the piece hanging under your right armpit but you can also strap it around your waist to where it hangs down on the left side opposite the cannon you pack. How many grenades you need?" He stepped over to a crate and rapped the top of it.

"Four." I hung the trench pistol over my shoulder.

"And some double 00 buck."

Willy's smile turned into a leer as he nodded, going over to the cabinet and pulled out a couple of boxes of shells then going to one of the crates and getting four grenades.

"How much?" I asked him as he bagged the stuff up in an olive green messenger bag.

"My treat." He chuckled. "Just cut the bastard in two for me."

"That I can do." Shook his hand and followed him back up, exiting the basement with him and as we entered the living room. Clare stood in the bedroom doorway, posing was more like it, her body encase in a gown so shear there was nothing hid. Both of us hesitated as we walked toward the door, me stopping to open it and Willy running into me.

"Are you sure you don't want to stay a while?" She had a wicked smile on her lips.

"Sorry kitten." I opened the door and stepped halfway out. "I've got business to attend to." She gave me a pout that was sexy as hell as I stepped on out the door, Clare giggling as it clicked shut behind me.

CHAPTER 18

Did I have a plan?

Yeah, I did but it could use some help before I headed toward my meet with Striker. No matter how you looked at it I couldn't go in there alone, the hoods would search me as soon as I stepped in the door and anything on me would be confiscated but that wasn't part of the plan, not even close. After going to Willy's, I headed to Kelso's and asked Fisk if he was bored. He grinned then asked me what I had in mind.

I told him what I wanted him to do and he nodded, then slid out of the booth asking when. I looked at my watch, one hour before I was supposedly to trade the notebook for Monica and keep Shelly safe. One hour. We walked back down to my office and I showed Fisk the trench pistol Willy had given me. He eyed it and a smile crossed his face.

"Pretty wicked hardware." He broke it open checked the shells then snapped it shut.

"Just don't kill Striker unless you have to." I pulled some Double 00 shells from my jacket pocket and handed them to him. "That mother is mine."

Fisk nodded as we went out to the car, crawled in and headed toward the Stedman homestead, neither of us talking as we drove. We parked two houses down from the place, walked up to the Stedman house in the moonless night, the wind blowing, biting through the gloves and making my hands cold. As we reached the house, Fisk cut off to the right, kept low and cut across the yard to the back of the house.

Once there he gave me a wave and in a crouch, moved across the back and to the opposite side of the house. I waved back then cut down the driveway side, a car was parked in the drive alongside the house, a big Buick with fender skirts and a shiny hood ornament, a nude woman that looked as if she was about to fly, Stedman's jalopy. I waited for a few moments, listened and looked for any signs of hoods on the outside.

Nothing moved in the stillness on the outside but through the window I could see a match flair, a cigarette glowed as it was lit, the glow reducing then dropped out of sight as the smoker breathed out smoke. I stepped up beside the porch, paused by the railing and peeked over it. In the window I could see a dark figure, barely visible, the cigarette flaring up again then going back to a dull glow.

It would have been easy to just take him out right then and there but then the element of surprise would be gone as I had a big surprise for them when Fisk got ready. I checked my watch, one minute then it would all pop. I mounted the steps and crept up to the door, keeping low so my body wouldn't silhouette the door window too much and waited.

At midnight exactly, there was a crash of glass breaking, the pop of gas grenades going off. Voices cussed, someone fired a shot, more glass breaking then the boom of the trench pistol, a scream, someone yelling to get down. I drew my foot back and kicked the door in as I lit a flare

Fisk had brought along, tossing it in the room as the door slammed open.

Biscayne had lied, instead of three there were five hoods, coughing and gasping for breath, tears running from their eyes as they turned toward the sound of the door crashing in. I should have gotten gasmasks but the damned things limit vision and I figured it wouldn't take long to end this with the tears flowing. I nailed the trench gun man first, his eyes not so teary, the muzzle of the gun swinging up. A second hood was on the floor, rubbing his eyes and aiming a pistol, I put one between his eyes, the top of his head popping off like the lid off a shook up pop bottle. From the room to my right the trench pistol boomed again, a scream echoing out into the main room, a body ran backwards then fell not moving, one side of his face ripped off. By now the gas was affecting me and I fired twice more at a couple of staggering figures, my slugs doing nothing but taking chunks out of the wall as another blast from the Ball Buster split the air and knocked the two down for the count.

I stepped outside, my eyes watering a little as the wind whipped up suddenly and blew through the house, the gas clearing out as it exited the busted bedroom windows. Fisk stepped out behind me, my .45 jumped up and then dropped when I saw it was him. His eyes were wet, the gas making him cough a little.

"The woman," he wiped his eyes, "she didn't make it. The bastard came into the bedroom and put a knife in her chest. I got him though, I think I blew his hand off but I couldn't tell for sure."

I nodded. People from the houses around were wandering out and rubber necking. I motioned for a burly fellow to come over and told him to call the cops. He said they already had. I showed him my ID, told him who I was, then told him when a detective Peterson got here to have him come to the hospital. I was going there. The man nodded as Fisk and I ran back to the car, jumped in and made tracks to City Hospital, hoping like hell we got there before Striker.

****

But Striker wasn't headed toward the hospital, instead, the little bastard had crawled in the back of my car, how he knew it was mine I couldn't guess or maybe it was just luck, but he was there, bleeding all over the backseat, his hand wrapped in a dirty rag that I had used to wipe the oil dipstick with, three of his five fingers blown off. We were in such a hurry that I failed to check, Shelly's safety foremost on my mind.

Just as we pulled out and headed toward town he popped up, a thin knife touching Fisk's neck his voice low, hissing like a snake's.

"You wish your friend to live, Ja?"

I jerked my head around, Striker looking at me, his eyes deadly, a sneer on his lips.

Out of the corner of my eye I could see Fisk easing the Ball Breaker down between the seat and the door his leg covering it to keep Striker from seeing it.

"No funny stuff, one move I stick him like the Italian Pig he is. You know where Miss Biscayne's house is, Ja?" he hissed looking at me. Fisk's face went red at that remark but he kept his cool. I nodded and told Striker I knew where it was.

"Good, go there." A slight groan came from him, his eyes dulled for a moment then brightened. "I should stick you now for this!" He held up his hand, the bloody rag dripped red as he shook it toward Fisk's face, his lips tight with pain and anger. He gasped then dropped the hand behind the seat, his mouth tightened as a bolt of pain shot through him. Fisk tensed as the knife drew blood then relaxed.

"No," he gasped, his eyes suddenly taking on a maniac's gleam, "I will save something very special for you."

He was breathing heavy, each intake of breath deep and each exhale long and shuddering, almost a death rattle. I hoped like hell he didn't die before we got there.

The Bitch's house was on South Street, about four blocks from the square. It was a big two story structure that had once been a hotel, then a boarding house, now a brothel. Striker told me to pull around back then said again nothing funny or he would slit the wop's throat. Fisk tensed again but didn't move, his eyes narrowing at Striker's comment but nothing more.

I pulled around at Striker's command and parked at the back entrance.

"Your pistol please, take the clip out first then toss it in the back with me." I pulled my piece out, ejected the clip, tossing it over with my .45.

"You have the notebook?" Striker asked pushing the point of the blade against Fisk's neck a little harder which made Fisk flinch. I told him yeah and he nodded.

"I told her I would get it for her, now she will reward me." His voice was like a little kid's, excited like when you tell one you have a surprise waiting for them. Only he got a surprise he wasn't counting on. Fisk's eyes jerked at the knife and I got his meaning, one that if it didn't go right he would be dead.

He jerked forward as I grabbed Striker's bad hand which was laid on the seat back, squeezing it hard and gave it a twist, the howl coming from his mouth more of rage than pain. At the same time Fisk handed me the Ball Buster, butt first, the hammers cocked as I raised the trench pistol even with Striker's head, the little shit froze, his mouth open and his eyes big as silver dollars.

"Boom," I whispered and pulled the triggers, both barrels going off, the noise deafening the both of us, the right side of Strikers head disappeared and decorated the inside of my car in gray matter, blood and bone. I tossed the trench pistol to Fisk who loaded it as he crawled out. Two of Biscayne's men bolted out the door as he slammed the breach shut, both of them catching a load each from the gun which knocked them back up the steps for only a second then they fell forward as I tossed the front seat forward and grabbed my .45, slid the clip in place and made for the door, Fisk right behind me.

I gave the door a kick and as it opened, two hoods were coming toward us, my .45 barked and both of them dropped like sacks of potatoes as I put lead into them, right in the chest dead center. The short hall we were in had three doors, two on the right and one on the left. The one on the right slammed open, Fisk grinned over the barrels of the Ball Buster as he pulled one of the triggers, the hood screaming along with the girl he was with as he was slammed back into the room.

Biscayne's office was the second door on the right, her name in gold letters. I stepped to the side, Fisk to the other and reached over and grabbed the doorknob, gave it a twist and shoved the door open, diving in and came up ready to end Biscayne's worthless life. Someone had already done it for me.

Biscayne sat slumped in her throne behind her desk, a hole in her head and the back of the throne decorated with her brains. I was about to turn to Fisk when he came in, Della Frost behind him nudging him forward with The Ball Buster.

"She caught me from behind." He shrugged as he stepped up beside me. Della grinned, her white teeth flashed as she laughed her face a mask of anger, madness and blue-black bruises.

"The notebook, where is it?" she snapped at me, poking the Ball Buster at my head.

""Easy with the thing lady." I pointed at my coat and

she nodded.

I opened my trench coat a little and started to get the notebook, then let the coat fall shut, her face suddenly bewildered as I locked eyes with her and raised my hand again.

"Question, Striker was your boy wasn't he?" Della gave me a lopsided smile then nodded her head.

"He was my lover." Her voice was soft but with a deadly tone to it. "Biscayne did hire him, but when he found out I was in town, he came to me to rekindle our old relationship."

"So when you found out what he was up to, you decided to woo him back into your good graces so when he got the notebook, the two of you could run this town."

"That was the plan, but you came along and well…" She pointed the Ball Buster at my head and took a step forward, both barrels looking like miniature caves.

"I heard Nora tell you about Vicky. She was jealous. She thought she and I were lovers but she soon found out that being my pet demands much more than the occasional slap with a leather strap. I was the one who carved the message in her chest and Fredrick was the one who sealed her flesh with the fire. Oh, we had quite a time with her, Striker in erotic ecstasy with each scream she shrieked.

"She nearly died but my sweet Fredrick brought her back, twice, then we sent her to kill the whore you live with and then once that was done and you were concentrated on her, Striker would kill you. You're a lucky bastard Mr. Black."

"So I've been told." I shrugged. She laughed again, this time a silky laugh that made the hair stand on the back of my neck.

"Did you know Russo has a thing for domination, nothing kinky, just the normal leather and lace bit? He'll pay handsomely for this notebook or certain pictures will be circulated among the families and Russo will be no more. Just as it is time for you to be no more Max."

Her eyes shined with insanity and her lips were pulled back in a lunatic's grin. I smiled back at her, her finger tightening on the trigger. Then that grin turned to surprise as I grabbed the Ball Buster and jerked it to the side, Della's hand dropping away from it as she staggered back, looking from me to the thin knife sticking from her chest.

"A little something your lover dropped in the back of my car." Della dropped to her knees and opened her mouth to scream, the rage on her face twisted it into something only a psychotic mind could manage. Then she fell sideways, her eyes losing their crazy and a thin trickle of blood rolled from the corner of her mouth.

"Damn Max." Fisk pulled a hanky from his back pocket and wiped his face. "I didn't think you were ever gonna stick that bitch."

"She wasn't close enough." I smiled at him. "I didn't want her to see it coming."

Fisk shook his head and stooped down to pick up the Ball Buster, looked it over and then let the hammers down easy.

"You have plans for this?" He held the Ball Buster out toward me and I shook my head. Fisk tucked it under his coat and walked toward the door, stopped and gave me a wave as he exited the room, the sound of sirens filled the air as I picked up my .45 and shoved it home, pulled out a cigar and lit up then leaned against Biscayne's desk and waited for the cops to get here.

CHAPTER 19

Well, after all the statements were given and all the falderal that goes with it, including a mob of reporters who screamed for the real story of what happened, Pat and I sat down in his office with the notebook, D.A. Wellman presiding. I grinned big when Pat showed him the page with his name on it; Wellman's face going pale, sweat popping out on it.

"You have nothing on me." He reached for the notebook; Pat jerked it back and shook a finger at him.

"Maybe not." He chuckled. "But I know a couple of boys who will be here to talk to you about it and they *will* be investigating the names listed in here."

"You son of a bitch." Wellman snarled at him. He pulled a hanky out and wiped his face as he stomped toward the door. He yanked it open and started out, two uniforms rising from the desks they sat at to block his path.

"Out of the way or I'll have your jobs!" Wellman screamed at them. He pushed his way through and headed toward the exit door just as two men in suits came through it, one of them flashed a folder while the other grabbed

Wellman by the arm.

"I've done nothing," he screamed as they hauled his ass out the door. "You can't do this."

Wellman really hadn't done anything except gamble in an illegal establishment and owe a known crime figure a lot of money. The others listed in the book weren't so lucky. Two judges, an assistant D.A. and six lawyers were listed as taking bribes. There were also a couple of county deputies listed for turning their heads where certain roadhouses were known to be distribution points for drugs and illegal cigarettes.

All in all, it was a pretty good bust for the feds especially since it had placed Russo in their cross hairs ready to pull the trigger and pull it they did. They nailed him at the airport making tracks out to a plane to flee the state. He almost made it too except one of the feds strafed the plane's engine with a Chicago Typewriter then fired another round at the tail section of the plane to which Russo and his boys gave it up.

I went to Monica and Ralph's funerals, stood back a ways and watched not knowing how the family would react to me being there. I really didn't have to worry. Monica's mother came up to me and shook my hand, telling me she thought she had raised her daughter right but she guessed she didn't take.

I took Shelly home a couple of days later. The hospital provided her a wheel chair (which was added to the bill) and fixed her up with a nurse to see to her needs while she healed. The woman came on a Friday while I was at the office. Shelly called and told me the nurse was coming down to see me. I asked what for and Shelly said it wasn't for the good.

I was still talking with Shelly when the woman walked in and guess what, it was the red head of whom I had tangled with at City Hospital. She tossed open the door, stomped over to my desk, well, Shelly's new desk and slammed a suitcase down on top of it, a nasty grin on her face.

"While I'm taking care of your girlfriend," she snapped at me, "you'll find another place to sleep."

I hung up the phone and leaned forward on the desk, my eyes locked with hers, a slight smile tuned up the corners of my mouth.

"I see." I nodded. "So does this mean I can't come to visit?"

"Oh, you can visit, but only on the days I tell you to." She leaned in toward me, her eyes drilled into mine. "For the life of me though I don't know what she sees in you."

"You don't huh." My eyes drilled back at her. "Well let me ask you this, how did she take it when you told her I wouldn't be around?"

"She told me she didn't like sleeping alone," Red growled at me. I let a wicked smile cross my face and Red's mouth dropped open and her eyes widened, her hand going to her mouth as she backed toward the door and out. I laughed, laughed so hard I fell out of Shelly's new office chair.

ABOUT THE AUTHOR

Author Ike Keen

Ike lives in the beautiful Ozarks, and is a member of many writing groups in the area. He's been writing for years, but this is his first attempt at a full length Mystery novel, and attributes its completion partially to one of those groups, Sleuths' Ink Mystery Writers. He prefers the old style of Mystery, and has adapted it to his writing voice. He hopes you enjoy.

Watch for the next two books in the Max Black series. Book two is called Bitch. You can only imagine how the plot will unfold.

www.ingramcontent.com/pod-product-compliance
Lightning Source LLC
Chambersburg PA
CBHW061212170626
46809CB00003B/1330